THE WINTER BEES

Behind each door of each small place in this collection
of ten short stories, people tend to their duties to keep
a small town humming. *The Winter Bees* introduces
seemingly mundane lives lived in a rural Minnesota
town and reveals journeys of personal discovery,
meaning, love, and hope.

Ana, the bartender, hosts Christmas parties for
children and raises money for charity, all the while
storing memories of her lonely past. Bachelor Hermann,
who pines for his best friend's wife, makes messes to
attract her over to his place and clean up after him.
The bookstore owner, Shirley, who neatly shelves the
stacks while longing for her dead husband, surprises
herself in a moment of cruelty.

These intertwined stories draw us into the everyday
lives of people whose duties often mean personal
restraint and heartbreak.

D0862152

THE WINTER BEES

THE WINTER BEES

by Jill Kalz

Minneopa Valley Press Inc.

Published by Minneopa Valley Press, Inc.
404 Moreland Avenue, Mankato, Minnesota, 56001, USA
www.minneopa.com

"Last Call" first appeared in *Minnesota Monthly*, April 1998. "The Flight of Herman Engelmann" first appeared in *American Fiction Volume 15* (New Rivers Press, 2016). Reprinted with permission

Publisher's Cataloging-in-Publication Data
Names: Kalz, Jill, 1968 - author
Title: The Winter Bees: fiction | by Jill Kalz
Description: First Edition. | Paperback. | Mankato, MN: Minneopa Valley Press, 2018.|
Identifiers: LCCN 2018954007 | ISBN 9781732208216 (paperback)
Summary: "These intertwined stories introduce seemingly mundane lives lived in a rural Minnesota town while revealing journeys of personal discovery, meaning, love and hope."
Subjects: LCSH: Minnesota—Fiction. | German Americans—Minnesota—Fiction. | Small town life Fiction. | German Americans. | German Americans—Fiction. |
Cover Art: Brian Frink, Poor Farm Studios
"Winter Hive" 2018; Watercolor, acrylic, 15"x22"
Cover Design: Bradley Coulter
Internal Layout and Design: Tawni Haukedahl
Design Consultant: Douglas Fliss
Printed by Bookmobile, Minneapolis, Minnesota, USA

ISBN: 978-1-7322082-1-6 (paperback)
Printed in the United States of America
First Paperback Edition, December 2018

For Mom and Dad, who wrote me into
their rural southern Minnesota
stories and gave me the tools
(including swear words in German—sweet!)
with which to write my own

"That's the story."

THE WINTER BEES

fiction

LAST CALL

*A*NA POKED HER HEAD OUT the front door, looked up and down the snowy street before shutting off the lights. She locked the saloon, climbed the warped back stairs to her apartment one step at a time. He hadn't shown up tonight, even though yesterday he told her that he liked sauerkraut and pork meatloaf, and certainly he couldn't turn down a fund-raiser for a good cause, especially if it meant cold beer, old-time music, and the chance to share some eats with a "good-looking woman."

Ana had been rubbing lotion into her elbows and forearms the first time he walked into the joint, a dead Saturday afternoon. He tipped his cap to her and smiled, settled onto the middle stool. "*Grüss Gott*," he said. "Got any Hauenstein?" His double chin bounced when he spoke, like some unsupported breast.

"*Ja, naturlich*," Ana said. She wiped her hands on her apron, pulled a bottle out of the cooler, and pried off the top.

He rubbed his knuckles, kneaded them warm. "*Scheisse, es ist kalt, nicht wahr*? Cold, huh? Guy shouldn't be out in this weather."

In her head, Ana quickly ticked through the possibilities. Traveling salesman? Visiting grandpa? A simple man without a map? "Supposed to snow more, too," she said. "The whole southern Minnesota is in some sort of watch or something till 10:00." She tossed a coaster onto the bar before setting down his beer. "Looks like we're right in the middle of it all. Montevideo clear down to Albert Lea."

The jowly old man took a large swallow and extended his freckled hand. "Lloyd Vogel."

"Ana," she said, then squeezed more lotion onto her arm. After a few careful circles, she looked back at the black-and-white football game playing above the bar. Long nights tending, mixing drinks stiff to speed the clock, had pulled her face down and cut deep lines around her eyes and mouth. She wore red lipstick, Woolworth's best 40 years ago. The gray knot of hair atop her head stood firm, severe as a fist. At the commercial, she dug out a Kleenex from inside her rolled sleeve and blew her nose. She noticed Lloyd staring at her elbows, or her low breasts, she wasn't sure which.

Ana tucked the tissue back up her sleeve. "I got psoriasis," she said. She wiped down the bar in front of Lloyd, talked to the wood. "And so I sent for this special lotion off the TV. Supposed to make it go away. But, ach—I don't think it's doing a damn thing." She set aside the rag and folded her arms, picked at the softened pink scabs.

The cooler motor kicked in.

"Say, were you a movie star?" Lloyd asked. His eyes narrowed. "'Cause I know I seen you before. Many years ago."

Ana shook her head.

"You look like Bette Davis," he continued. "Like you should have your name in lights. You've got Hollywood lips." He brought his fingers to his mouth and blew Ana a kiss.

She took a step back and scratched the underside of her arm, then looked up at the TV screen. Players lined up along the 35.

"No," she said. "But I wanted to be. I could'a been."

Lloyd followed her eyes up to the game. A long-dancing quarterback, an incomplete pass, and on jogged the special teams unit. "Well, you're certainly pretty enough now," he said. "And I bet back then you was some looker. Had all the men begging." Lloyd finished his beer, winked, and asked for another.

Ana smiled. The gold hooks of her partial flashed in the saloon's neon glow.

He showed up again the next afternoon. Ana shook a bucket of ice cubes into the bin behind the bar, plucked a few stray cubes off the floor mat and dropped them into the sink. "I had my portrait painted once by a famous artist," she told Lloyd. "Walter Eisenbauer. Said it turned out so good, he was going to show it in New York City. Said I was a natural model." She filled a green plastic bowl with beer nuts and slid it next to Lloyd's bottle of 3.2. "I'll maybe show it to you sometime. I got it upstairs, over the TV. I live up there, you know."

The bell over the front door jingled. Two regulars ordered the usual and hoisted themselves onto a pair of stools at the far end of the bar. Ana snapped off the bottle caps, adjusted her glasses on the tip of her nose, and counted out 50 pull-tabs. Lloyd tapped his finger on the wood in time with her count.

"So, what happened?" he asked. "You got married instead? Had the babies?"

Ana turned the channel, from an infomercial to bowling. One of the regulars thanked her. She took a swig from her own bottle of beer. "Someone had to take care of Ma," she told Lloyd. "Pa died. Johnny died. Someone had to run the place."

Lloyd looked over his shoulder, down the length of the bar, the back bar, into the grill area, Ana's face. "You're the only one that works here, then?"

Ana nodded. "*Ja ja, ja ja.* Lived here my whole life. Ma died just last year." She took another sip and pointed toward the tin ceiling with the bottle. "I got squirrels upstairs. Mean ones. I hear them up in the attic, making nests or something, looking for something to eat."

Lloyd leaned forward and lowered his voice. "Best way to get rid of them is to be nice to them," he said, "coax them out with a piece of good food, '*Hallo, my little squirrel friend,*' then POW! All done. *Fertig.*" He scooped a handful of nuts, chewed with his mouth open.

Ana laughed. "Catch them off guard, you mean, when they don't suspect a thing. You sure are a sly one, *gel*?"

Lloyd slid onto the middle stool every afternoon that week at the same time, just after the junior-high kids pulled their last pack of Camels from the vending machine, before the regulars shuffled in at 5:30 for the beef commercial special.

"You had a brother? Johnny?" Lloyd held his bottle like a prayer book. "What happened to him?"

Ana's eyes widened. "Johnny was in the war." She spoke quietly, deliberately, as though she were speaking about God Himself. "Over in Germany. He was a surveyor. Used to go and figure out where the shells would land, see. If they were too far in one direction, he would give them new coordinates and move them the other way." She gestured with her hands, moving them both left, right, then stopping in the middle, in front of Lloyd. "Until they got it right on target. Plenty dangerous work all right."

"So he took a bullet, then?" Lloyd asked.

Ana shuffled to the sink, ran water over a rag, and wiped down the faucet. Such a boy Johnny had been in the service, she thought, his uniform far too baggy in the shoulders, sleeves bunched at the wrists. The fair, soft face so eager to please still watched over her while she slept. Ana kept Johnny's army photo behind glass on her bedside table. Each night she touched a finger to his gray hand before closing her eyes. And each night she told him how sorry she was she hadn't been able to keep him safe—like big sisters were supposed to.

"Johnny brought me back a real Nazi flag he'd found. From a church steeple. I got it in the attic." Ana walked down the length of the bar toward the grill, each hand touching the wood, the brass, the wall for balance. "I'll make you a cheeseburger," she said without turning. "All week you come in here, and you never order anything to eat."

A thick cloud of grease and fried onions soon settled on Lloyd's shoulders. Ana watched him chew, watched the fat drip down his chin, onto the plate and bar. He sopped the small pools with his bun.

"*Schmeckt's*?" she asked.

He stuffed the rest of the burger in his mouth and nodded. Before screwing the ketchup cap back on, he ran his index finger around the bottle rim and sucked off the residue.

Ana cleared away his plate. "You know," she said, "I really don't know much about you."

"*Ja*, well, not much to know," he said, wiping his hands on the paper napkin. "Just an old Kraut who likes his *Bier* and likes looking at pretty things." He smiled at Ana. "Did that rat poison I bought you work?"

Ana rubbed her arms. "I think they're all dead but one. I still hear it late at night." She looked up at the ceiling. "I think it's waiting for the right moment to get me, you know, for killing its friends."

Lloyd coughed, took a swallow of beer, and coughed some more.

"You getting sick?" Ana asked.

"No, no, it's nothing." He pointed to the shelf behind her.

Her cousin Otto made tulips from wood, painted the square base, stem, and jagged leaves neon green, the blooms orange, hot pink, and lemon yellow. They lined the back bar, evenly spaced like obedient soldiers.

"How much for the flowers?" Lloyd leaned to the side and pulled a wallet from his back pocket, flicked through the bills. "Here's a $20," he said. "You pick the ones you like and put them in your windows upstairs. To brighten your day." He shoved the wallet back in his pocket and zipped his coat. "And the best part is, they will never die."

Ana tucked a stray hair behind her ear. "If you stay a little later tomorrow," she said, "you can watch 'Bandwagon' on the TV. Erwin Suess is playing. Starts at 6:00."

Lloyd tipped his cap and walked out the front door just as the regulars dragged in.

The opening strains of "Bandwagon" stopped conversations and hooked every eye in the saloon. The Saturday night "Bandwagon" meant polka, concertinas, and yodelers, all bouncing across Ana's screen in black and white. Flared pants, vests with "P.O.L.K. of A." embroidered on the back, the group home people who flailed their arms off-beat in the center of the floor or stared in the lens and swayed. Ana turned up the volume, made sure everyone had a drink, and leaned on the bar.

"That ribbon looks very nice in your hair there," Lloyd said. "*Ganz schön.*"

Ana raised an eyebrow. "You okay, Lloyd?" she asked. His eyes watered, the bags below them dark and puffed. "Your color's not so good tonight."

"Ach, *ja*. I'm fine. Probably just need another *Bier*."

Everyone in the saloon clapped along with Erwin Suess and his band, watched for names they knew and hollered when they found one among the lists of birthday and anniversary dedications scrolled across the screen. At 6:30, Ana turned down the volume, and most of the patrons closed themselves back into their own spaces. A couple of men at the bar played along with the "Wheel of Fortune" rerun that followed.

Ana replaced Lloyd's empty bottle. "Thanks for the flowers yesterday," she said. "I got them lined up on my dining room windowsill." She folded her arms and scratched the tops of the scabs until they turned white. "You know, Johnny didn't die in the war. He died when he got back." She paused. "Liver gave out."

Lloyd set down his beer and touched the sleeve of her sweater. "Oh, Ana, *tut mir leid*."

Ana blushed and quickly wiped her hand across her cheek. She looked up at the TV, called out consonants and bought vowels. She solved the puzzle four letters before the contestants did. At the commercial, Lloyd nodded toward a collection jar near the cash register and asked her about the fund-raiser for Tyler Matts, a grade-schooler who'd gotten hit by a snowmobile and snapped his neck.

"I'm cooking," Ana said. "Lots of German goodies. And Frank Nieman will play his concertina. You have to come. What else do you have to do tomorrow, on a Sunday night?"

Lloyd started to wheeze, so Ana poured him a glass of water. "A good batch of sauerkraut and potato dumplings, a little rye bread, will burn that cold right out."

Lloyd laughed. "Okay, you convinced me." He took one last swallow. "I wouldn't miss dinner with a good-looking woman for all the *Knödel* in the world." He pulled his cap tight on his head, his choppers on his hands. "And now, if I don't get going, I'll never get up in time for Mass tomorrow."

Ana tired on the third step to her apartment. So, Lloyd hadn't shown up. She had always hated that one thing the most about the saloon—the way people shuffled in, swallowed what she gave them, slapped a few bills, loose coins on the wood, then staggered back out for good. Over the years, some of them had wanted her to come along—out to a dairy farm, to Minneapolis, the Gold Coast of Chicago, Alaska. As she got older, fewer asked, so she tried going after *them*—to the edge of town, the pool hall down the block, the rusted screen door of the saloon. But one by one her joints stiffened. And her life stood still until someone settled onto a red vinyl stool on the other side of the bar.

Ana turned the knob and bumped open the sticky door with her shoulder. A couple lamps she'd left on in the living room welcomed her home. So did the warm, prickly smell of tonight's sauerkraut, its arms open wide. The woman staring at her from the portrait above her TV had long auburn hair, loosely curled, shiny red lips, and wore a buckskin cowboy hat. Ana couldn't see them from where she stood, but she knew they were there, those white, four-pointed stars twirling in the woman's pupils, the glint Walter Eisenbauer said he would take to the Big Apple. The head and shoulders of a girl who never dreamed a whole life could fit in one room.

Ana dropped her coat on the recliner and headed to the bathroom. Out of the corner of her eye she saw a flick of a tail, heard nails skittering across the hardwood floor. "You think you've come to get me," she said under her breath. She inched into the dining room and watched the squirrel grab hold of the wallpaper, scale one wall, crawl over the doorway, and climb back down. It made angry, *chit-chit-chit* sounds, jerked its tail as though setting a hook. "*Hallo*, my little squirrel friend," Ana sang. She slowly walked around the edge of the room, her eyes, unblinking, on the twitching animal, her hands feeling for her broom.

Suddenly the squirrel ran toward her, then leapt onto the wall beside her head. Ana grabbed the nearest thing she could find and swung hard, pinning the squirrel beneath it. The animal hissed and squeaked and struggled, scratching frantically as Ana pushed and pushed. Sirens and horns from the fire station across the street screamed through the windows and rattled the glass. Somewhere in the country, the wind was kicking a barn down to ash.

Finally, all the sounds stopped, and Ana pulled the plaster Virgin Mary statue away from the wall, let the dead squirrel fall with a thud.

She threw the body out the back window, washed her hands at the bathroom sink. Johnny's shaving kit still sat on the top shelf, along with a rusted can of Barbasol and a packet of new hankies, gold Js embroidered in the corners. Ana believed that as long as she kept something from each person she loved, parts of her life would never end, and she could go back to the beginnings and reread the stories she liked best. A teenage girl's lips would get her a screen test. A boy would come back whole from the war. A mother would lock her children out of the saloon and tell them to run far past the highway. The wooden flowers along the bar and sills would grow strong in the draft, fill the boozy air with seed.*

---

* *Reprinted with permission by* Minnesota Monthly.

THE HUMMING BEE

*T*HE KEEPER HAD TOLD *them at the beginning of the summer that he needed a favor. He had a friend who was sick inside, tired through her bones. Because the man was kind, the bees had obliged, spent most of their short lives gathering nectar from the clover blooming white along the Minnesota River.*

Joe Portner stood on the sidewalk, hands fidgeting inside his baggy pants pockets, while Shirley flipped the Closed sign to Open and yanked at the bookstore door. Although the sun had already been awake for hours, it just now rolled over the tops of the buildings across the street and stretched into Shirley's shop.

"Morning," Joe mumbled. He smiled her his yellow teeth and nodded.

Shirley squinted into the light. "Hello, Joe. How are you?" she asked.

"Good, good, got paid yesterday, so I gotta take a look at those books, those books I got on hold, lot of 'em, I'm sure there's a lot of 'em." He shuffled in, followed Shirley to the counter through a maze of tightly spaced bookcases and jutting display tables. The hardwood floor groaned with each step they took.

Shirley lifted a stack of books from beneath the counter, a rubber band tight around the pile. "I don't know, Joe," she said, raising her eyebrows. "I think I'm going to have to start charging you a hold fee pretty soon. What do you think of that?"

Joe grinned. "Oh, I'm gonna buy 'em, just a couple today, though." He touched the spines lightly with his index finger as if he were afraid of breaking them open, the pages spilling out like milkweed seeds. "This one here for sure, for sure this one, probably this one, too, for sure." His lips twitched. "Washed my hands today, this morning I washed 'em, washed 'em before I came in here for sure." He held up his palms for Shirley to see, fingers splayed.

Three times a week, Joe wandered into the bookstore and spent hours carefully turning pages, mumbling to himself. Always books about bees, honeybees in particular. Joe worked down at the railroad, had for more than 40 years, a hardworking grunt who wore his body odor and the grease and oil of the engines like a second set of overalls. Shirley had called him on it once, mentioned that he might want to shower more often, that it'd be healthier for him (and a bit easier on her nose). But sometimes he forgot. And on those days, Shirley just leaned back a little farther and kept him close to the open door.

"How much for this one, and this one, these two, how much?"

Shirley adjusted her bifocals, figured in her head, and gave Joe a number, $36, plus tax. The time was only shortly after 9:00, but humidity already thickened the air. Shirley could feel the covers of the paperbacks arching—smell Joe ripening in the heat.

He asked her when she'd be getting in some beekeeping magazines, and she gave him her usual answer: "Well, we'll see what we can do, Joe." He asked every time he came in, and Shirley didn't know whether he forgot during those days between visits or whether he believed that on one special day she'd say, "Just got this month's issue in today, Joe. And it's a fat one!" Most likely, he asked because it was part of the routine.

Shirley had tried to get him to talk about himself over the years—not the Bookstore Joe, but the Railroad Joe, the Frozen-TV-Dinner Joe she imagined, who holed himself up in his one-room house in Goosetown, every wall and level surface covered in books—but he never strayed from protocol. Rumors said Joe was one of the richest men in New Ulm. Adopted by late-in-life parents Delmar and Catherine Portner, young Joe supposedly received a fine settlement after the car crash that killed them both. That, in addition to the pay he earned at the railroad, and the money folks said the Portners had squirreled away early, knowing the challenges their beloved but slow son would face once they were gone, had set Joe well.

"I'll get those other ones there, those other ones next week," Joe said, "if you could just hold 'em, could you hold 'em for me, I'll get those next week for sure." He nodded and held his hand up in good-bye.

Shirley put the remaining stack beneath the counter and gathered up an armful of magazines to shelve. Joe's smell lingered like a party guest who had overstayed his welcome, and Shirley did her best to sigh and yawn and convince it to leave, all without much effect. She crouched by the magazine rack, pulled last month's issues and tucked the new glossy covers in. "Fifteen Ways To Tell Him It's Over." "Are Your Breasts As Healthy As They Could Be?" "Why Happiness May Lie In Your Man's Shoe Size."

Shirley clucked her tongue and turned to page 76. Happiness in the size of a man's foot, she thought. Her mother had always told her to watch for the size of a man's nose. The bigger the nose, her mother had said, the bigger the *Schwanz*. Shirley's late husband, Art, had had a strong Roman nose, and Shirley had had no complaints.

They'd met in 1960, in Shirley's hometown of Mankato, 30 miles south of New Ulm, both freshmen at Mankato State College. Shirley caught Art Reichman's eye as she crossed the campus square in her starched nurse's cap. Art snagged her heart and won her hand in marriage with his poetry. Although she never finished her degree—the sight of others' blood often made her nauseous—Art did, and after accepting a teaching job at New Ulm's public high school, he and his bride moved next door to his parents. The bookstore, a shared dream of Shirley and Art's, came later, when the children did not.

Funny, though she couldn't hear Art's voice anymore, she still heard the odd sounds he had made deep in dreams, his sigh after each sip of morning coffee. He hadn't really gone anywhere, she told herself, so it never was about missing him. The store was full of covers he had touched, pages he had breathed in, words he had rolled over and under his tongue like candy. The house, too, felt full. Sound construction had kept Art from stealing out around drafty sills and rotting doorjambs. Each night, Shirley still felt her husband's arms around her in bed. But she couldn't touch him back, and sometimes, in those quiet spaces before sleep, when her body finally yielded under the weight of arthritis and the long hours of light, that loss hurt her most of all.

"People truly will believe anything," Shirley said out loud, shaking her head. Her knees cracked as she stood up. The sound of her joints didn't frighten her. But the fast-moving blackness racing inward from the outer edges of her eyes did. The bookshelves, racks, and tables rapidly spun down a drain, and before she could throw out a hand to steady herself, before the words "I'm going to faint" could jump off her lips, Shirley's store vanished into black without so much as a gurgle.

It happened quickly. Shirley figured she came to seconds after hitting the floor. Her body was already trying to right itself and had pushed her to hands and knees. Her face felt wet and cold. She instinctively patted the floor, searching for her glasses, trying to center herself in a confused and blurry world. They hadn't broken, but something dripped and ran into her eyes. She knew it was blood, began to panic, and quickly called on "Other Shirley," her alter ego, the strong one, the one who'd been by her side when Art had seized for the last time and left her alone with all of those hard decisions and divisions.

Other Shirley helped her up, breathed steadily, and moved with purpose to the back room. She grabbed a dishtowel and pressed it to the gash above Shirley's left eye, pulled her a chair. And when Shirley frantically moved her tongue along the inside surfaces of her teeth—a tactile roll call—said she kept swallowing blood but couldn't feel any gaps, Other Shirley carefully touched Shirley's nose, gave it the slightest wiggle, and told her the floor had fractured it at the bridge. The cut above her eye, on the bone, had opened in a red spring on the edge of her lens. A few stitches, aspirin, and ice, and she'd be fine. Relax. Someone would be along soon.

Heels clicked on the hardwood. Stopped. "*Gott im Himmel*, what happened to you?" Rosadell Schroeder dropped her purse and rushed over to Shirley's chair, put a hand on her shoulder.

"I think I fainted," Shirley said. She stuck out her lower lip when she spoke, a fleshy dam to keep the blood inside.

"You look like hell. Here, we have to call somebody." Rosadell pushed the button on the Med-Alert box hanging from her neck. "I've had this thing for how-many years and never used it for myself. Always calling for you kids." She shook her head. "I hope to Christ you weren't trying to off yourself because of bad sales. Cleaner ways to do it, you know." She grabbed a newspaper off the desk and aggressively fanned Shirley with it. "*Honestly*. There *are* worse things in the world than a failing business. War. Droughts. Disease. Well, just think of all those abused dogs they show on TV. . . My God! And you're worried about a few books? Ach, what's wrong with you?"

Later—after Dr. Holtz had laid nine stitches just below her eyebrow and taken a few X-rays of her nose—Shirley took a good look at herself. Her left eye had nearly disappeared, the skin below and above it puffed out and stretched tight as sausage. The whole left side of her face throbbed, oozed purple and green beneath the skin. And her nose. . .so fat she wouldn't be able to wear glasses for a couple days.

Rosadell drove Shirley home from the hospital and threw her bloodied blouse and slacks in the wash to soak. Despite Shirley's protest, Rosadell insisted on taking the sharpest knives out into the garage and hiding them, thinking that if Shirley wanted to try to kill herself again, her "tools of death" wouldn't be so accessible. She'd have to put a bit more effort into it, and maybe by the time she uncovered them, she would've changed her mind. Of course this also meant that until she found them, Shirley would have to lift whole cuts of meat to her mouth on a fork and rip chunks off with her teeth.

Ben, a sweet preseminary student from the college in town who worked part-time for Shirley, called later that night and said he could tend the store until Shirley felt better. She appreciated his offer, but Heritagefest, New Ulm's annual German celebration, started in a week. Busloads of tour groups from across the country would be rolling in, all desperately seeking a little Germany in America. And they'd find it, or something close, in a snappy *Landejäger* and a cup of kraut, on the hem of a spinning dirndl, or inside the golden bell of a tuba. Shirley had all kinds of display tables and signs to get ready before then, radio announcements, the ad for the newspaper. The store depended upon the summer tourists and Shirley's sharp hand-selling skills to carry it through the rest of the year. Christmas helped, but without the fest-goers, Reichman's Books slipped into the red. If Shirley broke, the store broke, too.

She stayed up late, cutting out pictures of edelweiss and stacks of books—the scissors just inches from her eyes—and carefully pasting them into a five-by-five square. Squinting made her whole head throb, so eventually she gave in to the codeine and Dr. Holtz's order to rest. She dreamt until morning about her disconnected nose, concertinas and alpine horns, men's shoe sizes, and the warm, low hum of bees.

"Good morning, Joe," Shirley said. She unfolded a red tablecloth and draped it between a few props in the storefront window.

"Morning, Shirley, morning. I gotta see those books I got on hold, I'm sure there's a lot of 'em, lot of 'em back there." He grinned and scratched the top of his head.

The left side of Shirley's face was still puffy and yellow, her nose the dividing line between Before

Shirley and After Shirley. It had been five days since the accident, and she thought she actually looked worse now. The yellow reminded her of chicken skin.

"Heard you stopped in Friday, Joe. I bet you didn't miss me at all, did you?" She pulled Joe's stack of books from beneath the counter and rolled off the rubber band.

Joe laid the books side by side, hovered over one cover, then the next, almost as if he were smelling them, careful not to miss one letter or line of illustration. "I'm gonna get this one for sure," he said. His index finger tapped the cover twice. "For sure this one, not that one though, just these two, how much for these two together then, just these two, how much?" He looked up at her and smiled. There didn't appear to be the smallest sign of recognition that half of Shirley was the wrong color. Or that there was anything to be made of the get-well cards blooming along the tops of the bookcases, the vases lined up alongside the cash register.

After some quick figuring, Shirley gave Joe a number, which he then matched with a handful of coins and crumpled bills.

"Could you get in any of those beekeeping magazines, magazines for beekeeping, 'cause I looked and I couldn't find any and I know there's a lot of different ones, lot of 'em out there, but I couldn't find any here."

Shirley bagged Joe's books and tucked the receipt inside. A woman with a green fanny pack and matching visor walked in, glanced at the counter, and said hello. She did a double-take, thanks to Shirley's face, then started browsing the bargain bin. The fluorescent lights buzzed. Shirley's nose hurt. The codeine hadn't done much for her the past few days.

"Well, Joe," Shirley said, "we'll see what we can do. Not a big demand for those kinds of magazines. But, we'll see."

"Sure would appreciate it, getting those magazines, sure would be nice 'cause I know there's a lot of 'em, lot of 'em out there about bees. And they won't talk to me at the library, those people at the library, those people there." He scratched the top of his head again. "One of 'em stung me yesterday, bee did, one of my bees." His eyes fluttered. "Not its fault, though, no, not its fault at all. I raise bees you know, raised 'em for years, down by the river, along the river, and they're fascinating, very fascinating those bees."

Shirley nodded and watched Joe shuffle out the door and across the street, back toward the tracks. Her eyes watered from the pressure built up behind them, the pockets of fluid that her body hadn't absorbed yet. She didn't know if Joe had remembered to shower that morning, or the morning before. He looked cleaner, but she couldn't smell a thing.

Dr. Holtz told her the results of her blood tests were inconclusive.

"Meaning what?" she asked.

"Meaning, we don't know anything for sure."

"Well," she said, "then we've got some more work to do, don't we?"

For the next few days, nurses turned Shirley inside out. Pictures of her bones glowed on the office wall. Charts, equations, ratios, and codes spun before her eyes, fizzed and popped inside her ears like radio static.

Her appointments were wedged in between busy days at the store and long nights of insomnia. She was afraid to sleep. Her brain had stuck on one image and would not let go. Every time she closed her eyes, the same scene replayed itself over and over and over: the exact moment when her face had hit the floor. And *hit* the floor. And *hit* the floor. It was as though she were watching herself on film. A tight shot of her face smacking the hardwood floor. The crunch of bone. Snap. The fleshy slap of her cheek. Dead weight, 160 pounds, falling face first, with nothing to stop it but air. Sack of flour. Hit the floor. Hit. Hit.

Hit. That hard, varnished fist. And why won't it stop, this hitting that hits with a *stop* that hits with a hit with a *stop stop stop*.

Shirley stared at the ceiling. No sleep, no answers, and buses gliding down Minnesota Street, their bellies packed with shoppers, all looking for a piece of Germanic bliss.

Dr. Holtz flipped through the lab reports and shook his head. Shirley was in great health.

"Might have been something as simple as dehydration," he said. "Or a temporary drop in your blood sugar levels."

"That's it? I need to drink more water and eat a Snickers bar?" Shirley sighed. She was glad they hadn't found anything serious, but she'd hoped for something more specific, a concrete thing that she could point her finger at and say, "You did this. Shame on you!" Whatever had caused her blackout had checked in and out in a flash.

"I wouldn't worry about it," Dr. Holtz said. "I'll take another look in six weeks, see how you're doing, check that nose."

In six weeks, Shirley thought, the tourists would be gone, her "Discover New Ulm" tables replaced with back-to-school dictionaries and thesauri. Calendars and Christmas cards would start trickling in. The first 40-degree night would tease the storefront flowerboxes and threaten to steal their blooms.

"Ya'll have the quaintest little shop here," a woman gushed. "Why, it's just like I've been whisked away to Germany!" Her large hoop earrings grazed the puffy sleeves of her dress. It looked as though she were balancing two small rain clouds on her shoulders.

Every aisle in Shirley's store pulsed with costumed folks who had tumbled out of the motorcoach across the street. A round little man wearing a rhinestone crown (the Polka King) told Shirley they belonged to "Polka Partners USA, Arkansas chapter, a group dedicated to preserving the fine art of polka." The rain-cloud woman absent-mindedly picked her sleeves into bigger poufs and smoothed wrinkles from her sequined bodice while Shirley bagged her purchase. The Polka King's matching red jumpsuit flared at the legs. The white insets flashed with each impatient bounce.

Many of the men waited outside in a circle, wiped their shiny heads, and flapped their vests like wings while their wives browsed. The temperature was hotter outside, but at least the air was moving. Although Shirley hadn't seen him come in, she knew Joe had squeezed into one of the aisles. Her sense of smell had returned. And soon enough the Southern belles would smell Joe, too, through their thick layers of gardenias and spiced roses.

Shirley smiled, laughed, recounted her accident, and accepted sympathy until her face ached, thanked people for stopping in. She hadn't slept, really slept, in more than a week, and every morning she looked in the mirror and uttered one word: "ghastly."

She popped another codeine and washed it down with coffee. With the Polka Partners gone, the first lull of the day arrived. Shirley closed her eyes and prayed for the day to end. The heat, the steady stream of customers, the lack of sleep, the suspicion that her body wasn't as healthy as Dr. Holtz thought . . . everything blended together in a thick, nauseating hum.

"I'd like to put these two on hold, these two books here, if you could just add 'em to my pile there and I'll get 'em next time, but I'd like these two for sure, if you could hold 'em." Joe placed his books on the counter and shifted his weight from one foot to the other.

Shirley opened her eyes. Joe smiled his yellow smile.

"I'm sorry, Joe," Shirley said. "I can't hold books for you anymore."

Joe kept smiling. "Oh, I'm gonna buy 'em, just not today, if you could just hold 'em, and I'll get these for sure, these two and some of those other ones back there."

Shirley put Joe's stack of books on the counter, rolled off the rubber band, and spread out the titles. "No, Joe, I'm sorry. This is a business, and I need to have these books out on the shelves, so people can buy them." The narrow space between her eyes started to throb. "If you really want a book, you have to buy it today, or it goes back on the shelf."

Joe scratched his days-old beard. His eyes darted from cover to cover, to the walls, to Shirley. He tapped a book with his index finger. "This is a good book, and I'm gonna get this one for sure, for sure this one, I—"

"Joe," Shirley repeated, "if you want this one, you have to pay for it today, right now. I'm not holding them anymore."

He carefully opened *Hives of Joy* and stared at the illustrations printed in metallic gold ink on the inside cover. He tilted the book slightly from side to side, and it looked as though the bees were flying, dancing to music only they could hear. Joe cleared his throat. "If you could just hold this—"

Shirley slapped the cover shut. "That's it," she said. "This isn't a library, Joe. People buy books here. They don't put them on hold for months on end." She walked over to the Nature section and started shelving the books in her arms. Joe followed her like a toddler. "Nine books on bees," she muttered. "They all say the same thing, Joe. Each one of them. If you've read one, you've read them all."

"Fascinating bees though those bees, I've been reading about 'em, and—"

"Joe—"

"Very fascinating and if you could get some of those beekeeping—"

"Joe—"

"Those beekeeping magazines, sure would be nice to—"

"Stop it!" Shirley yelled. "Just stop it. I don't want to hear any more about the goddamn bees!" She shoved the last book into place and leaned against the bookcase, head down, one hand on her hip. She lowered her voice. "The world does not revolve around books and bees, Joe."

Joe's smile faded. He blinked repeatedly.

Shirley took a couple deep breaths, straightened up, and walked down the aisle toward the front door. Joe tagged behind. A few magazines had been stuffed back into the wrong racks on their spines, their covers curled out like tulip leaves. Shirley crouched down and tucked them back into place. And there it was again: "Why Happiness May Lie In Your Man's Shoe Size."

Shirley stopped.

What a circle she had made. Ten days and so much had broken. She was tired, the kind of tired that slips its poison into every cell, the toughest sinew and bone. Now was not the time to be making big decisions, she knew, but maybe she should think about passing all of this on to someone else, and soon. Work part-time. Ease up. Art had always told her not to get old on him, but that's just what she'd gone and done. Her days now were all about numbers, schedules, and racing the clock. Sales, inventory, cash flow, and profit margins. She couldn't remember the last time she had traveled somewhere for fun, or invited her girlfriends over for Irish coffee. She missed those things. She missed her husband. Time to be honest with herself: After 10 years, she couldn't hear the sounds he had made anymore. She couldn't feel him. These books weren't keeping him alive. The smell of the ink, sly and sweet, shared nothing in common with the warm saltiness that had lived within her husband's skin.

After a few minutes, Other Shirley helped her to her feet. Nothing spun this time. The afternoon sun beat through the yellow plastic over the front window, lit the store like 1,000 candles. And that's when Shirley saw the small glass jar sitting on the counter.

"Joe," she said quietly, "you have to go home now. I'm closing early."

Joe shuffled past, nodding his head, his eyes sliding from the floor to Shirley's face and back again.

He didn't say anything but timidly raised his hand in good-bye. Shirley turned the deadbolt behind him, flipped the Open sign to Closed as another swollen tour bus exhaled by the curb.

The bees had recognized a sense of urgency in the keeper's walk, one that hadn't been there before, an extra stutter in his song. They had filled their crops full and danced each other to the sweetest, most fragrant blooms. Their waxy homes had dripped and then thickened into gold in the wind their wings had made. And on a warm, July morning, the keeper had thanked them through puffs of smoke, wrapped their sticky gift in a small glass jar, and smiled them all a yellow smile.

A YIN-YANG YEAR

*B*EING UNDERWATER didn't frighten Luther. The color and sheen of the lake water comforted him, like bolts of algae-colored silk. He welcomed the cocoon.

But his heart tightened when he looked up to the surface, at the thick ice shell . . . when his cheek and hands skipped along its odd green underbelly . . . when his lungs blossomed, and he heard the surge and catch inside the lake's arteries.

He knew Minnie wouldn't let anything bad happen to him. If he just kept his chin level and let her lead, let the air bubbles float up like pollen . . . If he'd take her hand and pull the back of it to his lips, he'd be okay, and a slow thaw would begin.

Luther knotted his scarf at his throat, cinched his pants legs with rubber bands, and headed outside. Beautiful things had happened to his neighborhood overnight, things that Luther, a former high-school science teacher, knew were caused by dew points, cold fronts, and cloudless skies. His head prattled on and on, a looping internal lecture about the conditions necessary for hoarfrost. But his heart painted stars crackling and falling, landing on bare limbs, pine needles, every link in his neighbor's chain fence, and telephone wire that ran for miles.

Luther pedaled the three miles to Klein Manufacturing every weekday morning, regardless of the weather. Since his retirement from teaching, he worked in a quality control lab, testing powdered resins. The job was seasonal, which meant he worked nine months, then had three off, usually around February, when production slowed to a crawl.

During his free months, Luther invented things, conducted experiments, and packed his head with formulas and equations. His favorite idea, the one he hoped to turn into reality next summer, was to raise catfish in silos just outside Cedar Rapids, Iowa—a spin on hydroponic vegetables. Luther figured he'd seal up a few silos good and tight, fill them with nutrient-rich water, and watch his idea swim and multiply. It'd help alleviate the food shortage problem in the world, he told his skeptical co-workers. His Iowan fish would be distributed around the globe. Freeze-dried catfish. Frozen catfish burgers. Canned catfish stew. People laughed, but Luther knew his idea was gold.

One person who never laughed at the gems that lit up inside his head was his girlfriend, Marjorie. She worked at the library, in the children's section. In fact, it was during a story hour one Saturday morning that Luther had fallen for her. He'd stopped in at the front desk—along with what had seemed to be half the town—to pick up some books on inter-library loan. Giggles and squeals echoed in the hall that led to the children's section, and after a few minutes, a breathless boy popped in the doorway wearing a paper crown topped with a honey pot cut-out. The little prince scanned the long line at the front desk, then bounced in place and waved. "C'mon!" he cried. "It's starting!" The man in front of Luther waved back then turned his head around. "My son," he said. "Winnie-the-Pooh story hour." Luther smiled and nodded.

After checking out his books, Luther joined the huddle of parents in the back of the children's section, curious. He would never forget the way Marjorie said "bees," as in "You never can tell with *bees*." The word hung on her lips. He loved her flower-print dress, her long white hair, her red plastic glasses swinging from a silver chain, those sharp cheekbones, and the way she held her audience easily in one hand. At that story hour, Luther vowed that Marjorie Lendt would never again go home to an empty house. Every day after work, he biked to the library, walked Marjorie to her home four blocks away, and set a kettle of water to boil for tea. "Luther," she'd say, "you are such a sweet man. Please, stay awhile." And Luther would.

Luther's workday started at 7:00, though he always showed up around 6:15 and sat in the lunchroom with a cup of coffee and the local paper until the five-minute warning buzzer. People at Klein's didn't quite know what to make of him. New Ulm was a small, rural town, with men named Ed, Tom, and Bob. Maybe they had funny names like "Luther" in St. Cloud or Winona, Luther's hometown, but not here in farm country. He never dressed like the others, in grays and navy blue, opting instead for bold plaid, a size or two too small, pants belted halfway up his ribs. He wore lace-up oxfords, instead of work boots. He read books during lunch, instead of playing cards or griping about the falling price of soybeans. He had no interest in joining the company dart or bowling league. After he told folks he'd been a science teacher, they wrote him off as a kind of "Nutty Professor," thinking, perhaps, that a lifetime of chemical fumes had finally taken its toll.

"What's the good word this morning?" a voice asked.

Luther looked up from his paper. "Hey, Kenny. I was just reading here about our boys in Bosnia." He tapped his finger on the article. "I tell you, I don't see the logic behind it at all. Not at all. Sending them over *now*? Timing's all wrong."

Kenny worked in the resin production area. He liked Luther and was one of the few people who ever asked him to shoot a game of pool after work or stop at the Kegel for a drink. Luther's answer would always be the same: "Thanks much, kiddo, but I've got a little lady who'd crack my spine if I didn't show up at 4:00. 'Crack my spine,' get it? She works in the library, you know."

"Yeah," Kenny said, "'96 is gonna be interesting, for sure."

"It's going to be a 'yin-yang' year," Luther said.

"How's that?"

Luther leaned back in his chair. "Yin-Yang. Didn't they teach you that in school? It's the Chinese belief in the two halves combining to form the whole." He grabbed a pen out of his pocket protector and started to draw the ancient symbol in the margin of the funny page—a circle with two fat commas nested together inside. "See, yin," he said, coloring in one of the commas, "is the feminine part, the black half, usually thought of as dark, cold, and wet, that combines with yang, the masculine part, which represents light, heat, or dryness, to create all that comes to be in this world."

He looked up at Kenny and grinned. "It's going to be a good year."

"But what does that have to do with 1996?" Kenny asked.

"Well, just look at the '9.' Then look at the '6.' Obvious, isn't it? Yin/Yang, 9/6?"

Kenny rubbed his forehead, then reached for Luther's pen. "But wouldn't it have to be 19*69*? You know, with the '9' and '6' reversed?" He wrote the numbers next to the yin-yang symbol and chewed on the pen cap. The five-minute warning buzzer sounded.

Luther shook his head and sighed. "Oh, you're right. 1969. *That* would've been a yin-yang year." He sat and stared at the paper.

"I didn't mean to burst your bubble or nothing, Luth. I'm just saying, you know."

"No, no, you're right." Luther put his pen back in his pocket. "You are most certainly right, Kenny. I got my numbers mixed up there." He folded his newspaper, chucked Kenny on the shoulder with it, and walked toward the lunchroom door. "You have a good day now," he said.

1969. The year melted onto Luther's brain that morning and stuck hard. No matter how he tried to distract himself with temperature testing, particle sizing, and moisture content analysis, he couldn't chip that year out of his head to save his life.

Many people believe there's one person in the world who's their perfect match, their soul mate, the one person who would make life absolutely complete. Whatever they lacked, the soul mate would provide; whatever the soul mate lacked, they'd make up for in spades. For Luther, that person had been Wilhemina Olson, "Minnie" to her friends and family.

Minnie and Luther grew up in Winona, Minnesota, just across Front Street from each other, not far from the Mississippi River. Minnie— the mayor's daughter—was three years older than Luther, but they'd always been best friends. Smart, and a tomboy, she was one of the first girls in town to cut her hair short like the boys, "short," she'd say, "like Amelia Earhart."

"Dutch," she said one day walking home from school (she called Luther "Dutch"), "you know what I'd like most in the world? More than anything?"

Luther shifted Minnie's books to his other arm and shrugged. The year was 1939. He wasn't quite 12 but already had a strong sense of the manners you were supposed to show a girl (carrying books, holding doors, walking streetside), even if it was just Minnie.

"To sail across the seas in a great steamer," Minnie continued, "and visit Rome and Greece and Africa and the Far East." She ticked off each place on an invisible chalkboard in front of her. "I want to take an expedition to the North Pole. Or the South Pole! I want to be a scientist and find cures for the diseases in the world." A brown dot overhead caught her eye, and she tipped back her head and sighed, watched a hawk glide in a fat, lazy O. "Well, *I* couldn't do that," she continued. "That'd have to be you. I'm simply awful at chemistry. But *you* could do that." Minnie's face glowed, and in her excitement, she walked past her own house. Luther followed alongside.

"There's so much out there, Dutch. So much I could be. And I want to see it all!" She threw out her arms and twirled on the ball of one foot—likely the most girlish thing Luther had ever seen her do. "I don't want to just read about it. I want to build my own ship and float down the Mississippi, all the way to the Gulf of Mexico." She twirled again, and a handful of sparrows exploded like buckshot into the trees. "I want to live on a faraway island, fly around the world, write like Shakespeare."

Luther stopped walking. Minnie did, too. But she wasn't quite done talking. "I want to shoot up into the heavens and land on Saturn's rings and see if there's life up there. We could do it, Dutch. We could. You build the rocket, and I'll fly it. Like Amelia Earhart. Only much better."

"It'd never work," Luther said, looking back at their neighborhood.

"Why not? 'Cause I'm a *girl*? That's hoo-ha, Dutch, and you know it," she said with a huff. "Girls can do anything boys can do. In case you forgot, I beat you and every other boy in town at broomball."

"It just wouldn't work," Luther said again.

"Don't you think I'm smart enough?"

"No, that's not it."

Minnie glared. Luther was in love with her already. Her glare, even though it was meant to scare him to the grave, gave him wings with which he flew over the little river town in great circles and across the Mississippi to Wisconsin and beyond. He simply loved being near her. She had made it clear, without having ever said so, that she thought of him more as her younger brother than a beau, but Luther continued to dream. He made sure he walked her home from school every day, keeping a keen eye out for competition, though all the boys in town thought of Minnie as one of them. She fished, played football, wrestled, went joyriding, and sneaked cigarettes with them behind Fusillo's Store. If anyone ever needed help with his hook shot, Minnie was his answer. And if anyone ever needed a good introduction for his theme paper, Minnie was his answer again.

"Okay, *Luth-errr*," Minnie said, still glaring, hands on her hips. "Why wouldn't that work?"

Luther stammered. "Because—well—because the rings are made of rocks, chunks of ice, space debris, that type of thing. The rings—they—they aren't solid—and—therefore—there'd be no surface on which to land." Luther could feel the heat rise to his cheeks and into his ears. The corners of his mouth sagged.

Minnie bent backward and shouted to the sky. "See what I mean? You're so *good* at that science stuff.

If you don't become a great scientist someday, I'm going to find you and kick you to the moon!" She gave him a playful push that nearly landed him and their books in the levee, ran a hand through her cropped, blond curls.

They walked another block before Minnie said, "Hey, we walked right past our neighborhood."

"I know," Luther said.

"Why didn't you say something?"

Luther shrugged. They walked a couple more blocks until they were within sight of the park.

Minnie cried out, "Last one to the band shell is a rotten carp!" and tore off. Her skirt waved at him like a loosened sail.

"Hey!" Luther shouted. "No fair! I'm carrying all the books!"

"Aw, what's the matter, Dutch?" Minnie called over her shoulder. "Can't beat a *girl*?"

Luther gave chase but let Minnie win. It was enough for him to know he *could've* beaten her, especially since she was the one who had given him wings.

A couple years later, in the summer of 1941, James Murphy arrived. James was a naval man from Boston, the son of one of the mayor's closest friends. He was tall and lean, had a bright smile and a wicked laugh—and Luther hated him. The Olsons had invited James to stay for 10 days, a short leave before he had to return to duty. Minnie, who was the most unshakable person Luther knew, stuttered around James, kept smoothing her hair and pulling at the short curls. She stopped swaggering like one of the boys and starting moving inside her clothes like water. She avoided the baseball diamond and the fishing hole, opting instead for a soda downtown or long walks with James along the river. The worst part? Minnie introduced Luther to James as "my little adopted brother across the road."

Luther wanted to run away, run until he collapsed, until he coughed up every memory he had of Minnie, just so he wouldn't have to look at her, with *him*. But he couldn't run. He couldn't do much of anything but sit on his porch, or up in his bedroom window, or in the crotch of the front yard elm, and watch. He'd hang back as Minnie and James walked to the park, then hide behind the clubhouse and listen to the slow back-and-forth squeak of the tandem swing, their laughter and Minnie falling in love.

Minnie and James married six months later, in mid-January. Luther went to the wedding, danced with the bride, and congratulated the groom. His family gave the couple some china place settings. Luther gave Minnie his own gift: a model rocket he'd designed and built himself.

After the wedding, James returned to his ship in the Pacific, and Minnie stayed with her parents. One frigid February morning, she spotted Luther out shoveling the sidewalk, called his name, and waved him in.

"Hot dog," she said, "it's too cold even for the snowmen!" She took his coat and hung it on a hook by the door.

Luther thanked her, removed his boots and cap, wiped his dripping nose with a hankie from his back pocket. "I don't mind it so much if it's not windy," he said. He stood a bit hunched and avoided looking directly at her lemon-yellow dress, instead sweeping his eyes from the floor rugs to the plastered walls and ceiling of the sitting room. Neither he nor Minnie said anything for a few moments. A cuckoo clock kept Luther's pulse.

Finally Minnie threw her arms out at her sides. "Well, welcome!" she said, beaming. "Have a seat. I just made coffee."

Luther sat gingerly on the edge of the loveseat. Minnie and a whisper of violets sat next to him. She poured two steaming cups, black, then bumped a little whiskey in each from a silver flask pulled from her pocket. She looked sideways at Luther as if sharing a secret. They clinked their cups and took a sip.

"Mother lent me the sitting room until James and I get our own house," Minnie said. "We got so many gifts from the wedding, my bedroom just wasn't big enough."

What was once the Olsons' formal sitting room was now half sitting room and half pregnant loading dock—wooden steamer trunks and crates stacked along the walls. The loveseat, coffee table, two accent chairs, and two end tables formed a colorful, warm island in the middle of the room.

Minnie gestured to a couple crystal vases, an inlaid cigar box, a porcelain figurine of a blond woman in a sweeping mint-green gown. "I put out some of the nicest things, so I could enjoy them. No sense in keeping *everything* packed away. Especially since I don't know when James will be back." She took a long draw on her cup.

Luther shifted slightly on the loveseat, subtly scanned every shelf and tabletop, squinted to see through the glass of the curio cabinet standing against the far wall. And because Minnie had known him forever and could navigate his heart blind, she patted his knee and added, "I'm saving the *best* gift, though, for when we move, and I can make my own true home." She dipped her head around into Luther's line of sight and caught his eyes. "I'll find the perfect spot for your rocket, Dutch," she said. "Promise."

Luther exhaled and smiled, his lips pressed together tight. Such a luminous word, he thought: "promise." He wrapped it in tissue, nestled it inside the quiet rafters of his heart. "Thanks, Minnie," he said at last.

Over the following few years, Luther and Minnie still talked and joked around with each other, but they didn't go fishing like they used to before Minnie married or walk to Sugarloaf Bluff in hopes of catching a glimpse of its legendary 14-point buck. They saw less and less of each other, and their friendship faded, as so many childhood friendships do. After the war, James came back for Minnie. And in a flurry, she was gone.

Luther and Minnie never wrote. Luther didn't ask for her address and figured she was too busy with her new life to write to him. He later heard that she and James had lived in Japan, Bangkok, and Saigon, where she'd taught English to Vietnamese women. James retired a captain, and Minnie realized many of the dreams she'd shared with Luther that day in Winona.

    In early 1969, the yin-yang year, James and Minnie returned to the United States. Three months later, while skating on a frozen lake behind their Oregon home, Minnie broke through the ice and drowned.

Luther floated through his workday, cushioned from the buzzers and timer bells and co-worker chatter, as though he were suspended in a deep, warm bath. Kenny caught up with him at the employee exit at 3:00.

"Missed ya at lunch today." Kenny cupped his hand to his face and lit a cigarette. "Me and the guys are getting a game of broomball together tonight up by Five Fish Pond. Around 6:00 or so. Perfect night for it. Wanna come?"

"Thanks, Kenny, but—"

"I know, I know, Marjorie'd 'crack your spine.' S'okay. I get it."

"No, no," Luther said. "I just . . . that sounds fine." He unlocked his bicycle, pulled his cap down over his ears, then steered the wide tires south, toward the library.

Luther knew Marjorie was worried. He hadn't said more than 10 words on their walk to her house. Usually he had so many ideas swimming in his head that he talked nonstop, barely letting her get in the necessary "Uh-huh," "Oh, really?" and "What a wonderful idea!" She asked if something had happened at work earlier. He shook his head and looked out toward the street. Once inside Marjorie's bungalow, Luther walked into the kitchen, filled the teakettle with water, and set it on the stove. Marjorie hung up her coat and reached for the cribbage board on the top shelf.

"Luther, how about a game?"

But Luther was already at the door, his coat, scarf, and hat still on. "Marjorie, I'm sorry. I have to go."

"Oh," she sighed. "Are you sure you won't at least stay for a cup of tea? It'll warm you up. It's awfully cold out there."

"Thank you, dear." He pecked her quick on the cheek. "But I just really have to go."

Marjorie stood in the doorway and watched him crank the pedals of his clunky old bike. "Thanks for walking me home!" she called. "I'll see you tomorrow!"

Luther's white and black socks flashed back at her, one on each side of the red steel frame, up then down, in a meter reserved for the slowest of waltzes.

Dinty Moore beef stew was the best Luther could do for supper that night. After the fourth mouthful, he scraped his plate into the garbage and set it in the sink. His stomach turned.

He had rented his apartment furnished. Only the dishes, a couple lamps, a roll-top desk, and his personal items belonged to him. A block of windows on the east side invited the sun in every morning to slide across the walls and inside the curve of the doorway arches, the wide lines of the ceiling. But by the time

Luther came home from Marjorie's, the rooms turned cold and close. He found himself breathing in shallow, quiet breaths, as though there wasn't enough air left in the apartment by sundown, as though taking a deep breath might suck the walls in even farther.

He looked toward his darkened bedroom and thought he saw a steamboat crawl downstream. The view from his second-floor bedroom window in Winona had always made him feel as though he were in the crow's nest, high atop the mast, keeping lookout for signs of trouble. From his childhood room, he could see the long twists of smoke rising from every chimney, the individual shingles on Minnie's house, the calm pulse of the Mississippi, and where he'd be when he died. He'd always known that, at least since he was a teenager. And no one in his family, not even his father, scoffed at that. They'd all known where their end would be—his grandparents, uncles and aunts, his parents, his little sister—and they'd all been right.

Luther popped four antacids, bundled himself in winter gear, and pedaled to Five Fish Pond.

No more than eight feet at its deepest, the pond held nothing but mosquito eggs, algae, and an occasional duck during the summer. In winter the ice teemed with schools of figure skaters. Luther biked to the opposite corner of the park, where a manmade rink glowed beneath banks of white light.

"Hey!" one of the goalies yelled. "We got us an audience!" He motioned toward Luther settling himself in the bleachers.

Every head turned. Luther waved.

"C'mon out, Luther!" Kenny called. "Ya gotta help me! I need someone who can actually *play* on my team here!"

"Naw, I wouldn't want to make you all look bad!" Luther yelled back.

A collective laugh slid across the ice, and play resumed. It was a perfect winter's night—no wind, no clouds, nothing but pin pricks of light from the corners of constellations. Everything seemed clearer: the outline of Sebastian Woods, the edges of the bleacher benches, creases in the players' jackets, even the grommets in Luther's shoes. The sub-zero air rushed inside Luther's throat and chilled him from the inside out. His nose started to run. The cold was the good kind—not the kind that froze your skin, but the kind that cooled it, bit it, until you were conscious of every pore, every small hair.

Players zoomed past Luther's bleacher. Brooms and bodies flew. White puffs of breath rose from the rink like smoke signals. Blue, red, and stripes of yellow blurred on the ice. The sideboards cracked but held under the weight of body checks and slap shots. A warm smell collected above the game and drifted into the park—the smell of sweat, dirt, beer, and a wood-burner a mile down the road.

Luther woke an hour before his alarm the next morning. He knotted his scarf, cinched his pants legs, and headed outside. Night was draining behind Sebastian Woods and Five Fish Pond, and by the time Luther biked past the park, the sky glowed ice blue. For the second morning in a row, the temperature had taken a dive, and hoarfrost coated every tree, hedge, wire, and basketball net. Halfway to work, Luther doubled back to the park.

The game's heat from the night before had long since crystallized, but Luther could feel the shifting shapes of the players still moving about. He slid across the rink in his oxfords and passed shots to the ghosts. The *shhh-shhh* of Luther's shoes and a distant industrial fan were the only sounds awake at that hour. He continued to warm up and practiced quick stops and evasive maneuvers.

Then he saw her standing at the opposite side of the rink, broom in hand.

"All you have to do," she said, "is get one little goal off me. Think you can do that?"

Luther untied his scarf, took off his hat and gloves, and threw himself into a fierce game, a one-on-one with the only person who'd force him to play his best. She pushed him, checked him with her broom, and led him around the rink until he started to cough. He leaned against the sideboard to catch his breath, tried to curb an oncoming cramp. The sun inched between the pines. The ice seemed to light up from underneath. Luther couldn't believe how beautiful his world could be. Even the rink lights were haloed.

"Hey! Wake up!" she yelled.

The ball sailed at Luther's head. He blocked it. She was on him again.

Luther gripped his broom tighter and pressed hard down the middle of the rink, panting. She hung on his heels. The goal was open. He took a shot. No good.

"You're playing like an old man, Dutch!" she called and sprinted down the ice for an easy goal.

Luther charged and stole the ball back. He kept it close, the broom's bristles tapping each side of the ball in a blur. She spun circles around him, no matter how fast he went, how tricky he tried to be. Before he could say, "What the—," her broom batted the ball away and into the opposite net.

Luther's face burned. His chest tightened. Ice droplets formed in his nose. He wasn't going to let her beat him again. He had waited too long. He gritted his teeth and flew after her. She saw him coming and smiled.

"Now," she said, "that's more like it."

The problem was, Luther slid too fast and couldn't stop. He slammed into the sideboard with a thud. Every bone in his back cried, "You're 68, for Christ's sake. Go sit on the bench!"

She skated over to him and asked if he needed any help, if he was willing to forfeit. Luther swallowed hard. He shot up, stole the ball, and yelled, "Aaaaahhhhhh!" He hammered it toward the opposite net. Score!

"Ha!" he shouted. "I did it! I did it. I scored off you, and don't try to tell me you let me win, either, 'cause I won. I won fair and square, Minnie!" He shook his broom high in the air and spun around to face her.

But Minnie was gone. Luther scanned the edges of the rink, the bleachers, and the warming house area. Nothing.

He bent over at the waist, closed his eyes, and took slow, deep breaths. He cupped his nose and mouth with his hands until his fingers were wet. True, he'd beaten her, but he hadn't won. He was alone on the ice, bare-headed and cold. And after work, and after walking Marjorie home, he would return to his apartment, where he would sit alone and watch the walls inch closer together. He'd always known it: When Minnie left Winona, and even more so when she died, Luther knew there would always be a dark, comma-shaped part of him trapped in a deep freeze, a part that would never thaw. Everything he had come to care about most in his world—the river, his hometown, the dreams he had had about changing the world—was so special because he and Minnie had shared it together.

Luther straightened up and shuffled off the rink. He walked over to Five Fish Pond, leaving his bike behind, and slid out to the middle. His toes prickled. The sun nudged the pine trees aside and lit his face. The moisture hanging in the air caught the light and threw it back like millions of mirror chips.

Bending his knees, Luther slowly lowered himself onto the ice, a hand out to catch his weight, and lay back as if he were going to make a snow angel. A few blocks away, a semi downshifted. Luther lay still and filled his lungs with winter air. Moments later, the ice spidered in all directions beneath him. His heart fell. The mercury in every thermometer along the Minnesota River Valley fell that morning, too—but not nearly as far.

Marjorie looked out the library windows again at 5:00. Maybe, she thought, the day was just too cold for Luther and his bicycle. It hadn't been this cold in years. Such a deceptive cold, too. The sun had been shining, and everything sparkled, but the man on the radio said any exposed skin would freeze in minutes. Maybe Luther had a flat tire. Maybe he was home sick. He hadn't seemed himself yesterday. Or maybe he'd decided he was happier on his own and didn't know how to let her down easy. Maybe he had fallen too fast asleep.

The three library chimes rippled through the periodicals and kissed Marjorie's ear. She pulled the collar of her coat tight under her chin and headed home alone.

THE FLIGHT OF
HERMAN ENGELMANN

I USED TO FARM A STRETCH just outside Essig, in Milford Township, and for the last six years before I turned it over to my nephew and moved to this apartment here in New Ulm, I kept up a strip of grass right down the center of it. Sixty feet wide, 500 feet long. A runway for my buddies. The WingDings— that's what we called ourselves; a bunch of crazy nuts and their radio-controlled airplanes. Oh, a couple younger guys drove out once in a while and flew helicopters and all sorts of strange contraptions—one joker from Sleepy Eye even built a flying pancake, pats of foam-core butter on top and all—but most of us flew warbirds: Corsairs, P-39s, Zeros, Spitfires. Like we always said, "Bigger flies better."

Women had no place there. Not that we went out of our way to discourage them from coming out, understand. But it was easier when it was men only. Simple. Comfortable. When a woman showed up on the flying field, it was like turning everyone's transmitter to the same channel—and waiting for all hell to break loose.

I loved to fly, especially my Sukhoi. Aerobatic plane. As soon as I finished mowing, fixing the chisel plow, hauling grain, or doing whatever else needed to be done for the day, damn if I wasn't heading out to the flying field with my girl. I'd fuel her up and dance her into the sky. I had routines that changed with the weather. Blue skies lit a fire under my ass, and I looped and swooped that plane to the snap of Herb Alpert and the Tijuana Brass. We didn't have a sound system out there or anything, just a makeshift lean-to we could sit under for some shade when we weren't flying. But I heard the trumpets clear in my head as soon as the wheels lifted. Same as I heard Louis Armstrong on those partly cloudy days, the ones with little wind and the high cirrus clouds, when I'd turn on the smoke, and arc and dip and fly through my own white rings. She flew so effortlessly. Made a guy forget his body had weight, that he wasn't sitting up there beneath that canopy.

Just like a woman, the Sukhoi had a mind of her own and did what she pleased, no matter how I sweet-talked her. Had a few minor bumps over the years— crunched the landing gear once when she caught a bad crosswind coming across the corn, busted more than a few props, all repairable stuff—but I lost her altogether right after Doc's hip problems took a turn for the worse. One minute she was winking at me in the light of a September evening, and the next, she was barreling full-throttle into the ground.

Doc Johnson and I had grown up just down the road from each other. We'd gone to 12 years of Catholic school together, farmed neighboring fields for more than 40 years, and we were both members of the WingDings.

That's where our similarities ended.

Doc was a crotchety son-of-a-bitch. Tight, too. Always tracking things to the penny. Whenever it came time to split the tab over at Smiley's after a day of flying, he'd get out his pen and start figuring on a napkin, trying to divide some cheese-bread, a couple pizzas, and a few pitchers of beer five ways, though he didn't have any cheese-bread, he'd tell us, on account of his high cholesterol, so he didn't think he should have to pay anything toward that, and he'd had only one glass of beer all night, making his share for the pitchers proportionately less. The bill at Smiley's never amounted to much over $40 anyhow, so eventually, after watching Doc carrying the ones and rounding up to the nearest cent for a good five minutes, one of us (usually me) would figure the hell with it and just pay the whole thing. And you know, he never once offered to cough up the tip. How he ever conned Lila into marrying him, I truly will never know. Couldn't have been his looks. Man was uglier than a mudfish. Never knew what she saw in him that the rest of us didn't.

I was the bachelor farmer of Milford Township, which meant I got invited to plenty of folks' holiday gatherings and had other guys' wives bringing me helpings of beef roast, fried chicken, and stuffed pork chops during planting and harvest seasons. Not a bad deal. Jerry's wife, Joan, was always good for a few batches of homemade kraut in the fall. Edwin's wife, Dot, kept my cellar stocked with jars of plum and apple jelly, pickles, beets, squash, and pumpkin. Frank's wife, Phyllis, as round as she was tall, could be counted on for pans of bars and a couple rhubarb or caramel apple pies. And Doc's wife, Lila? She'd stop over with some cleaning supplies once a month and whip my place into shape. We'd tell each other jokes and talk a bit about the local news—who'd died or gotten ticketed for speeding, the drop in corn and soybean bushels, how the New Ulm boys were bound to choke at State again this year . . . that type of thing. The house always looked, smelled, and felt better after she'd been there.

"Jesus, Herm," she said once, scrubbing the burner pans in a sink full of suds. "All I'm asking you to do is maintain. Just once, couldn't you make potatoes without letting them boil over?"

I was sitting at the kitchen table, flanked by newspapers, airplane magazines, and a set of paints, working on my latest treat from the hobby store: a new pilot for my Corsair. Not all my planes had pilots—some didn't have enough clearance beneath the canopy, even though a pilot isn't much more than a set of shoulders and a head, and some just looked better without them—but I thought the Corsair deserved one.

I shook my head. "I ain't got time to sit and watch water boil, woman. I got a farm to run here, you know."

Lila looked over her shoulder at me, hands still in the dishwater, eyebrows raised. "Oh, but you've got time to sit at that table for an hour, trying to get just the right shade of red on your little doll's lips there."

"That's different."

"Yeah, that's different, alright."

Lila could run circles around me in the smarts department—no question, one of the sharpest gals I knew—though she never made me feel less than I was. That said, I do think she kind of enjoyed knowing she always had one up on me. That's why, whenever I had a chance to needle her, I did. Just for a rise.

"And, by the way," I said, showboating a little, "she's a *pilot*, not a *doll*." I set down my paintbrush. "Geez, Lila, I'm disappointed in you. Get the terminology right, would ya? Haven't Doc and I taught you anything over the years?"

"How can she be a pilot with no arms and no legs?"

"She's a handicapped pilot. There are handicapped pilots, you know. This one, well, she steers by wiggling her torso."

Lila turned. The sink drain gargled behind her. "Are you sure she doesn't steer by wiggling her *boobs*? That's quite a set she's got there."

"Really?" I said. I tipped my new pilot back and forth in my hands, fingered the hard plastic bumps. "I hadn't even noticed she *had* boobs. Huh."

"Ach," Lila said, slapping my shoulder with a wet yellow glove, "*you're* a boob."

The screw in Doc's left hip started worming its way back out in November 2005, the day before Thanksgiving, and the screw in the right hip did the same in December, on Christmas Eve, while Doc was helping unload presents from the back of his son's truck. The pain of two loose hips dropped him to the snow like a heavyweight punch. They were 10-year hips, the doctors had told him back in '93. Doc, of course, being Doc, got his money's worth and managed to sneak in a couple extra years. But time was up now, so the family hauled him into the emergency room, where he was poked, doped, pricked, X-rayed, and then wheeled back out to the truck with an appointment card for surgery and a less-than-happy "Happy Holidays" from a nurse who'd pulled an unlucky shift.

A month later, when they opened him up, the son-of-a-bitch was all soured inside, full of infection. Doctors claimed they'd never seen so much pus. They took out the left hip but kept the right one in. It wasn't as far gone yet as the left, and I suppose they figured the man needed *some* way to move around, at least a little bit. They certainly couldn't put the new hips in with all that infection, so they scraped and scrubbed everything clean as they could, sewed him shut, and soon after started him on 45 days of antibiotics. Pills *and* shots.

Fool should've gone into a nursing home, where he would've had trained people taking care of him— that's what the doctors said, too. But nursing homes cost money, see. So instead, Lila got some quick lessons from the hospital staff on how to change dressings, how to handle a syringe, how to roll her husband so she could change the bed sheets, how to move his legs so the muscles didn't get all spongy. She also learned where to support him so he could get out of bed and across the hall to use the toilet, how to keep his pain in check, and how to monitor everything that went into Doc's body and everything that came out. Doc's two boys loaded their dad flat on his back into the older son's truck, drove him home to the farm, and laid him on the bed. And on that double bed, staring at the ceiling, is where Doc Johnson stayed for the next 45 days.

Lila stopped over at my place the second week of February, cleaning supplies in tow. I hadn't seen her since before Christmas, before Doc's hospital adventures began, and I was beginning to wonder if she'd just stop coming by. After all, taking care of Doc was a full-time job when he had two *healthy* hips. I couldn't imagine the work it took when the guy had one missing and another with popped hardware. And really, in the dead of winter, when I wasn't out in the field and all I had to do was build and repair airplanes on my kitchen table, I should've been able to keep my own house clean. Parts I did—in general, I kept it picked up and made sure nothing smelled too bad. But I was glad Lila came by. I'd missed her.

"Word over at Smiley's is you and Doc won the lottery," I said, "and you've been holed up, filling cream cans and plotting where to bury them once the ground thaws."

"Actually," Lila said, unwrapping her scarf and brushing off the snow in the doorway, "we haven't even been home. We've got body doubles living over there at the house. Doc and I have been partying down in the Bahamas since Christmas." She rolled up the sleeves of her turtleneck, exposing forearms white as the snow she'd just brushed off. "See my tan?" she said with a wink.

She walked right over to the kitchen sink and started filling it with hot water. Bubbles puffed out of the soap bottle and floated to the ceiling like tiny pink pearls.

"How's the patient doing?" I asked, getting back to the wing I was sanding.

A cupboard door thudded. Then another. "Fine," she said. "He pretty much just lies there. Does a lot of crossword puzzles, holding the magazines up over his head. Has to use a pencil, though, because, you know, pens won't write upside down."

"Need those NASA pens, like the ones the astronauts use."

Lila pulled out the stovetop burners and looked at the crusty drip pans. She scowled at me and dropped the pans into the sudsy water. Then she opened the oven, pulled out all the racks, and coated the inside with white foam. "I'm just going to let that sit for a while," she said. "I don't know what kind of explosion you had in there."

"Oh, that would've been the lasagna," I said. "Made myself a treat for New Year's. Garlic toast and everything." I picked up a finer gauge sheet of paper and continued sanding. "Used the wrong pan, though—too small—and that tomato sauce and cheese just bubbled out all over the place. Boy, what a mess."

"I see that," Lila said. She picked up her tote of cleaning supplies and walked behind my chair. "I'm going to make a quick pass through the bathroom. Any explosions in *there* I should be made aware of?"

"No, I try to keep that pretty clean."

She patted my shoulder. "Good."

"Say," I said, raising my voice once Lila left the room, "you going to the WingDings' party over at Carl's Saturday night?"

"Doc's not supposed to go out while he's on his meds," she yelled back. "So, no."

"Well, *you* can still come. Have a beer, talk with the wives. Food's always good, and you have to eat anyhow, right? I'm sure they'd put together a to-go box for the patient."

I heard her spray more white foam—a different white foam—all over the shower doors and tub. I heard her lift up the toilet seat and squirt bowl cleaner around the rim. Then came the frantic squeaking as she scrubbed the water spots and flecks of toothpaste from the mirror. She ran water, wet a sponge, and wiped it across the tile, the shiny chrome fixtures, and the shower doors she'd sprayed—the soap scum already lifted and carried on the bubbles' backs. I heard the stiff bowl brush, the flush, and the gurgle. I heard the mop slap the crackly linoleum. But I didn't hear Lila say anything.

I stopped sanding and, with my voice raised again, said, "So, what do you think about Saturday, then?"

After a long pause, Lila flipped off the bathroom light, walked back into the kitchen, and said, "I'll think about it."

Nothing beats broasted chicken, baked potatoes with sour cream, and bottles of Schell's on a cold February night. Carl set us up in the back half of the dining area, even pulled out the paper placemats with the red poinsettias in the corners, seeing as how it was supposed to be our club's Christmas party.

Before the meal, my buddy Dean showed some of the video he shot last summer: footage of the WingDings out at the flying field, some from his trips to AirVenture and the air races out in Reno.

'Course I'd forgotten to bring along the screen like I said I was going to, so we tried projecting right onto the wall. Carl's is covered in wood paneling—that real dark-brown stuff—so that made it tough. Then Dean taped a bunch of placemats together. Worked pretty good, though every once in a while someone's plane nosedived into a poinsettia, just like a hungry bee.

No one mentioned Doc and Lila until we started passing around the dinner rolls.

"It's gotta be bad over there," Joan said quietly. "But you know Lila. She won't say nothing."

Dot clucked her tongue. "Woman's going to work herself into an early grave, that one is," she said. "I tell you, I wouldn't do it. Waiting on that man hand and foot. She's a prisoner in her own home. Can't even leave him long enough to get her hair done, for Christ's sake."

"Come on, Dot," Edwin said slyly, bumping her shoulder. "You saying you wouldn't play nurse if I was laid up like that?"

"If you were as ornery as Doc, hell no." Dot coated her roll with a thick layer of butter. "Have you ever heard that man say one kind word about her? Ever? And it's not like they don't have the money to pay for home health care. Oh, they have it. Doc just won't part with it, is all."

"When's he go see the doctor again?" Jerry asked.

"March 10," I said.

"And what happens then?"

"From what Lila told me, if his blood work looks okay, they'll schedule him for surgery down in Rochester."

Dot shook her head. "I'll bet Ed's left nut this is not going to end well."

Edwin set down his knife and fork and leaned back in his chair. "C'mon, now," he said. "Why bring my sack into this?"

"Pfft," Dot said. "It's not like you need that old thing anymore anyway."

A few days after the party, the weather turned nasty—nastier than we'd seen in years. A foot and a half of fresh snow, followed by highs in the teens, *below* zero. The entire state was a neglected freezer, every building frosted over like an old TV dinner. Like everyone else, I stayed in. I made a double batch of chili, fiddled with the engine I'd been building, and watched plenty of "Andy Griffith" reruns. And I watched the calendar, too, hoping March would roar in with good news for us all.

"What's this?" Lila asked, accepting the large rose from my hand as I let her in.

"They had a deal at the Holiday station this morning," I said. "Buy a dozen donuts, get a free rose. Some sort of St. Patrick's Day special."

Lila paused. "Well. Thank you. Don't often see roses like this . . . neon green . . . edged in silver glitter." She tipped the flower side to side, curious. The petals caught the light like a disco ball. "Do I get a donut, too?"

"A what? Oh—I ate them all."

"Herman Engelmann, you ate a dozen donuts for breakfast?"

I held a straight face as long as I could, just to see her cheeks flush, then broke into a grin. "No," I said, "I gave a few to the gal behind the counter—real nice gal—and then I ran into Edwin and gave him a few for him and the wife, so no, I didn't eat them *all*. No. Geez. What do you think?"

Lila snipped a bit off the stem and stuck the rose in a tall glass of water. "Well, good," she said. "You eat 12 donuts, and you'll be bound up for a week."

I sat back down at the kitchen table and started paging through my latest issue of *Sport Aviation*. "I'm just happy Doc's finally going to get that surgery," I said. "June'll be here before you know it, so . . . Been a tough haul for you. For Doc."

Lila set the makeshift vase on the counter, pulled out a chair, and sat at the table with me. That was my first clue something wasn't quite right. She never did that—never sat down when she came over.

The clock ticked. The fridge hummed. The pages of my magazine crackled as I flipped them, ads for landing gear, flight schools, and camshafts buzzing for attention. Lila folded her hands on the table, carefully stroked each dry, reddened joint.

After a few minutes, I leaned back and switched on my portable radio. "KNUJ's even getting all Irish today," I said. The radio popped and spit before a pair of concertinas squeezed their way into the room. "Heard it in the truck this morning. I don't know. Do we really need a 'Danny Boy' *polka*? Sometimes those fools over in New Ulm just don't know when to leave well enough alone."

Lila cleared her throat and resettled herself in her chair. "Say," she began, still focused on her fingers, "remember a few weeks back, when we had all that snow and then the god-awful cold?" She didn't wait for me to answer. "Well, I mean, who doesn't remember that? Of course you remember that. Everyone remembers that. It just happened!" She looked long out the window over the sink, toward her house, then at the bold flower on the counter. "I tell ya," she continued, "I felt really stuck inside. Inside the house, I mean. And then when I went outside, with those five-foot drifts alongside the garage?" Her eyes closed, and she shook her head. "Cripes, I felt—I felt stuck there, too, ya know? Stuck. Couldn't move. Couldn't breathe." She opened her eyes and looked across the table at me, really looked. "There was nowhere to go *in*side, and nowhere to go *out*side. Just—well—there was just nowhere to go."

The words hung in the air a bit, then settled on our shoulders.

And just like that, the space between Lila and me shifted. So quick, so slight, no one sitting with us would've noticed. Like a twitched finger on a stick and the resulting tick of the ailerons that takes a plane off center and rolls her left. I'd known Lila more than 40 years, but at that moment, I didn't know what to say.

Thankfully the radio announcer spoke up for me. He read the station ID and told us that even though the local temperature was 25, with the wind chill it felt more like 1.

This is the beauty of Minnesota: Fewer than two months later, the corn was in, and I was out at the flying field in jeans and a T-shirt, putting up flight after flight till the sun told me to stop playing, go home, and make supper. Lila had come out to the field a few times since the start of spring to watch me and the other guys fly. I brought along the trainer, thinking she might like to learn how to fly herself. I offered a number of times, but she always shook her head. I told her if she was afraid of losing a finger flicking the prop, I'd show her how to use my chicken stick. No shame in it. I still used it once in a while. She waved her hand at me, urging me to shut up and take off so she could sit back and enjoy a good show. We didn't talk much about Doc. In fact, she rarely mentioned his name at all.

Since St. Patrick's Day, Lila was stopping over at the house at least twice a week—barely giving me time to get the place dirty between visits. I found myself bypassing the rug by the back door just to leave muddy boot prints on the linoleum; making my frozen pizzas without a pan so the cheese would ooze through the racks and cement itself to the oven floor; and brushing my teeth wide-mouthed for the biggest spatter pattern on the medicine cabinet mirror.

I knew why I was doing it: I didn't want Lila to feel like she was wasting her time. Like I said before, the place felt lighter and brighter after she'd been there. The air smelled fresher because of the soaps and disinfectants and the perfume she wore.

But I'll be honest now. It was more than that. My messes gave me excuses.

Of course Lila has to come over, I told myself. I'm a schluppy bachelor farmer who can't keep his pots from boiling over or the lime from choking the holes in his showerhead. She's doing me a service, helping out an old friend, making sure I don't become buried in my own filth and trigger a batch of rumors throughout the township. She's *not* coming over to escape her life at home, I assured myself, to get away from Doc and his demands. She's not coming over because she feels anything more for you, you tired old fool, than friendship. It's the messes and her need to clean them up that brings her by. I make my many messes to give her something to do, to give her reason to come talk smart and keep me on my toes. I do *not* make them so I can pretend we're together, pretend she's chosen me and I've chosen her, pretend the rest of my days will start and end with her. Because that would be wrong. *That* would be *wrong.* And thoughts like that could only hurt a man.

I had to hear myself say it out loud, so one morning after she'd finished vacuuming, I said, "Say, Lila. Does Doc know how often you come over here?"

"Why?"

"Well," I stammered, "I—I just don't want to cause any trouble or—get in the middle of anything. Know what I mean?"

"Doc always knows where I am," Lila said, winding up the vacuum cord. "I tell him when I'm coming over. There's no sneaking going on, if that's what you're worried about." She wheeled the vacuum into the hall closet. "You and I are just friends, Herm."

"No, I know," I said. "Sometimes I just wonder if Doc—"

"And besides, with the surgery coming up next month, I'll be sticking closer to home, helping Doc recoup, and you'll have your house all to yourself again. No one to keep putting down the toilet seat."

"Probably better for me to sit anyway," I said. "Aim's been for shit lately."

Lila smiled. "Speaking as the woman who cleans your bathroom, I can vouch for that. Good thing you don't *fly* as off-target as you *pee.* They'd be finding pieces of balsawood all over the county."

That evening I drove east to New Ulm. The Legion was sponsoring a Made-Right Night, and I hadn't been to one all year. I ordered three sandwiches with the works (ketchup, mustard, pickles, and raw onions), a bag of chips, and a Diet Pepsi. And I started talking to a woman at the bar nursing a rum and Coke—a widow from town named Shirley. I made her laugh, and she touched the back of my hand. Before I knew what I was doing, I asked her to join me for dinner at the Kaiserhoff the next night. A date. My first date in more than 20 years.

None of us could believe it. But 10 days after Doc's surgery, his sons were racing him back down to Rochester, fever boiling his blood and straining his every seam. The doctors opened him up, and in the cool of the O.R., infection hissed like a snake.

So out came the new left hip, the old right one, and with them any chance of Doc walking again. No matter what the doctors gave him, no matter how much or for how long, Doc stayed sour through and through. Guess that's just the way he was meant to be.

His boys started building the ramps as soon as he came back home. They said Doc didn't want any visitors, so I just watched from my kitchen window— the loads of plywood, the hospital bed delivery, Lila running to the store—until the corn got too high for me to see anything below the Johnsons' second floor.

I flew a lot that summer, took advantage of the hot, dry weather to test out a few new planes, catch up with the rest of the WingDings, keep my mind off Lila and the things I imagined going on in that house. Doc's boys said their dad sat on the front porch a lot in his wheelchair, watching our flights, but that when they asked if he wanted a ride to the field, he shook his head and grunted. He said no one wanted his crippled ass out there, said he didn't want people looking at him funny and feeling sorry for him.

I never brought Shirley out to the field. In fact, she came out to the farm just once. I always met her in New Ulm for our dates. She didn't seem very interested in flying and referred to me and the guys as "you boys and your silly toys." But that was okay. I liked having my own hobby with my own friends. I'd been alone for so many years that it was tough for me to find a balance between time *with* Shirley and time *without*. She was a sweet gal, but I think we both knew we wouldn't last long.

"Hello, stranger," Lila said, standing on the step. She held her tote of cleaning supplies with one hand and a pan of chocolate-covered bars with the other. "Been awhile, so God only knows what you've done to the place. Thought I might need reinforcements: fresh batch of Special K bars. Already cut."

"Come in! Come in!" I said, holding the screen door. "But you know you're not supposed to do labor on Labor Day. It's a law or something."

Lila set down the tote and pan on the kitchen counter and did a quick sweep of the room with her eyes. A fly buzzed past her head, darting to the window glass, the ceiling light, the clock. "Looks good!" she said, hands on her hips. "I'm impressed, Engelmann. Although I'm also a little hurt. Doesn't look like you need me anymore."

"Well, I wasn't sure if you were coming back, so . . . It's true. I'm trainable."

"I never doubted."

"How's Doc doing?" I sat down at the table, my newest warbird—a brilliant blue Bearcat— commanding the entire surface, and considered which decal to put on next. "I sure was sorry to hear the news. Just awful."

Lila sighed and started unpacking her tote. "He's angry. Bitter. The boys and their families are over visiting, so he's not quite so owly today." She tapped the pan of bars with her index finger. "Want one?"

"Yes, please," I said. "You take one, too."

She nodded. "Once I'm done cleaning," she said, plating a square and bringing it over to the table for me. "The meds help with the pain, which is good. But he's getting more and more depressed. I'm sure I'd feel the same way, knowing I was never going to walk again."

I took a couple bites of my bar, watched as she pulled on her yellow gloves and filled the sink with suds, her back to me. The fly bounced repeatedly against the screen door. I hesitated a moment, then asked, "You thought at all about getting him into a nursing home?"

Lila chuckled. "You know as well as I do he'd never leave the farm. Plus, he's my husband, you know—bum steer that he is. For better or worse."

"Well, sure," I said, licking chocolate off my fingers, "but that doesn't mean you have to give up your life for his, does it? I mean, no one ever sees you anymore. I never see you anymore. You never get out—"

"I get out plenty."

"Out, sure, to get groceries, to pick up Doc's drugs . . . What about coffee with the gals? Or going shopping? Just laughing and having a good time?"

Lila rinsed a glass and carefully placed it on the drying rack. "Listen, I've got a man at home who can't take a shit without me. I've got two grown boys who don't know how to act around their own father anymore. Me having a good time is the last thing on my list right now."

"I'm just saying—"

"I know what you're saying—"

"I'm just saying you have to get yourself some help. You're a tough bird, Lila, no doubt about that. But you can't do it all yourself. No one could."

Lila took off her gloves and turned around to face me. Hard lines drew down the corners of her mouth. Her look took me in with a chill. "You know," she began quietly, "I envy you, Herm. I do. To be able to pick and choose the parts of life you like best. Avoid the work of it. Run away from the messy parts. You want to spend your days in the clouds, you can. Whatever Herm wants to do, Herm does. You aren't responsible for anyone except yourself." She folded her arms. "You don't even have a goddamn dog."

I looked down at the table and nodded. She was right. "It's just—I just wish things were different for you," I said. "That's all. I—hell, I don't know."

Lila shook her head and covered her eyes with her hand. "No, I'm sorry. I'm sorry." She exhaled. "I know you're trying to help. I think I'm just overtired. You got anything to drink?"

And that's when she noticed the photo on the refrigerator door.

"Who's this?" she asked.

I waved the fly off my plate. "Oh, that's Shirley and me at the winery," I said. "Shirley Reichman. Owns a bookstore over in New Ulm. We've been sort of dating the past few months. I haven't had a chance to tell ya." Lila kept staring at the photo. "I don't know what possessed me to ask her out in the first place, 'cause, you know me, I don't do that. I never do that. Me going out on dates . . . Crazy. Crazy stuff. But I asked her and she said yes, so Widowed. No kids. Nice gal. Smart, too. When I hug her, you know, it's just like I'm hugging you."

The moment the word "you" came out of my mouth, I regretted it, and regretted it bad, wanted to fly it right back down my throat. I fumbled the controls. "What I mean is—"

Lila turned back to the sink and pulled the plug. She wrung out the dish rag.

I started again. "What I mean is, you're both basically the same size—short and small—and so when I—"

The drain gurgled. Lila rinsed the sink, draped the yellow gloves over the faucet to air-dry.

I couldn't level her out. "Lila, I don't want you to think I pretended That's not what I—"

She continued to stand at the sink with her back to me, looking out the window at the corn now bled of its green, looking at the rooflines of her house and outbuildings rows and rows away.

"I can't come over anymore, Herm," she said finally.

I slid back my chair and stood up. Lila packed up her cleaning tote, slow and steady, and walked to the table. I'm not sure how long we stood there, unable to breathe, the air between us thick and heavy as exhaust. It could've been a couple minutes. Maybe an hour. I honestly don't know.

I wanted to tell her I loved her. Should've told her I loved her. I should've stopped her at the door when she looked at me that last time, the smallest, tired smile trying to break. I should've held on tight when she said she'd choose me if she could, if things were different, if it wasn't already far too late. That's what I should've done.

Instead, I said nothing. Did nothing, except let her walk out the door and close it behind her.

I should've stayed inside after the last of the dust kicked up by her truck slipped into the corn. Should've drank myself into a long sleep, so I'd have had time to catch my breath, fix the parts inside me that weren't working. I should've stayed as close to the ground as possible.

Instead, I grabbed my Sukhoi and headed out to the flying field. I put her up fast and snapped her, rolled her, pushed her inverted into countless spins. My hands shook. No wind. No sound except the whir of the engine.

I watched her but didn't really see her until she winked, a flash of deep gold light off the canopy. Then she flew straight up, the red star on her tail soaring. I hadn't touched the elevator and frantically tried to correct, get her out of the climb. She hesitated, stalled, then turned toward the ground. Dead stick. I shook the radio and watched, helpless. "No, no, no," I prayed as she dove fast into the corn and shattered.

I live here now, in New Ulm, about 10 miles east of the old farm. Sold the land to my nephew shortly after harvest last year. I'd been meaning to get out of farming for a while anyway—body can't do what it used to, you know—and the stuff with Lila just sped things along. The WingDings took most of my planes off my hands. Not much room in the apartment. They wouldn't let me sell them all, though, said I couldn't get out of the club *that* easily. And they made sure I didn't wait too long to put up another flight after I lost the Sukhoi. Gotta get back on the horse, they said.

They talk about Doc once in a while at our meetings, and I might catch a little news about Lila. Not much. I think about her a lot, wonder what she's doing at different times of the day, what she thinks of me now.

Sometimes, on clear summer mornings, early, before the sky slips sure into pink, before the day's first ethanol train whistles through the valley, hugging the river, I'll walk to the end of the block, lick the tip of my index finger, and hold it up in the air to check wind direction. Old habit. And more often than not, she's blowing from the west.

BLUE BIRD OF HAPPINESS

VIRGIL FISHED OUT A LACY GARTER from under the bench seat with his broom. Pretty thing. Small. Ivory netting with ivory lace, the thread blushing. He thumbed the blue satin bow, then stuffed the garter inside his jacket pocket.

He continued sweeping, shooing candy wrappers and spent petals out the back of the bus. At least he wouldn't have to use the hose this year. Last year's bad chicken turned some prom-goers inside out. There were plenty of tears. Not just the girls. Boys, too. The Behnke kid sat and laughed. Vegetarian, of course. So Virgil made him help wipe down the seats, threw a roll of paper towels at his head, and told him to stop being such a dick. He got in a little hot water for it later, Virgil did, but he felt it was worth it to see that kid, in his tux, sopping up a mess of meaty vomit while trying to hold back his own eggplant lasagna.

Virgil gassed up the bus, drove it back inside the garage, and headed home. Once there he let Butch out to pee. Nighttime bus runs always set Virgil buzzing. Something about the light the kids gave off, their fluorescent hum, the weight of carrying them—

all that valuable, bright cargo—on the rows behind him. The retirement job kept him young. Most of them really were good kids, the younger ones tugging their parents' sleeves, breathless, at the grocery store, saying, "That's Virg, my bus driver!"

Butch whined, and Virgil let him back in. The two settled on the couch, turned on the TV. Virgil cupped the dog's head, tennis-ball small, and scratched behind his ears, told him tomorrow they'd go out to the lake, see if Uncle Mike had gotten his dock in. Butch nosed Virgil's jacket pocket and snorted.

He should've dropped the garter in the lost-and-found box. Over the past eight years, Virgil had turned in a handful of cell phones and textbooks, countless mittens, a few lunchboxes, scarves, keys, a flute . . . He'd kept a nearly new knit cap with the school's screaming eagle on it. That winter had been particularly harsh, so he wore the cap, wore it a full week to warm his bald head when the wind bit down, thinking someone would claim it. No one did. And Virgil was happy about that.

He rolled up his pants leg past the knee and slipped the garter over his foot and halfway up his calf. The elastic bucked. He tried coaxing it, small tugs to keep it from rolling belly up, but the garter dug in hard and couldn't be wooed.

Virgil turned his leg from side to side, asked Butch what he thought. The lamplight loved the sequins. Virgil smiled.

A few minutes later, he pushed the garter back down his leg and marveled at the bright-red ring on his skin, his cool temporary tattoo, while Butch leapt off the couch to lap at his bowl.

THE SIEBENBRUNNER NOSE

*E*VERYONE RECOGNIZED THE NOSE, that grand, hooked beak Greta had always tried to hide. She had grown her hair long, tipped her hats low, pointed her face down, down, down to the ground, chin to chest . . . but that insolent nose had loved attention and turned people's eyes like a ruffled girl in ringlets. And today was no different. Powdered and pink, it sat high on Greta's face, savoring the mourners' sympathy like hard candy.

"I wouldn't'a recognized her if it hadn't'a been for the nose," an old classmate said, juggling keys and coins in his coat pocket. "Definitely a Siebenbrunner, *gel*? The rest of her, though, don't look like her at all. 'Course I ain't seen her in a long time neither."

Neither had Greta's sister Eleanor, even though their homes were just a mile apart. But she had called Greta once a week, spent the 15 minutes discussing when the tomatoes needed to be picked, the earliest glad bulbs could be started, whether Greta had entered KEYC's annual "Predict the First Snow" contest. Greta won once, the time they gave away a year's worth of dry dog food, courtesy of Horst's Ag

Supply. Five hundred pounds of kibble delivered all at once to her front step one Saturday morning. Last year's contest winner received his likeness carved in a block of butter.

Eleanor had had her suspicions.

"So *what* if she's eating it?" her husband, Ray, had said. "Can't be that bad for her. Thing is, your sister made her own bed years ago, and now she's got to lie in it. Don't you go feeling sorry for her. Don't you do that to yourself, Norrie."

Greta had made no secret of turning her back on God after her other sister, Frieda, had died. Greta blamed Him for stealing Frieda away and never set foot in church again. "They'll have to carry me back in," she often said.

In light of that, Eleanor felt good about her choice not to hold a full funeral mass at St. Mary's, opting instead for this small prayer service at Henle's Funeral Home. Besides, most people who had known Greta were either already dead or soon on their way, tucked snug into nursing homes. Most of Eleanor's children and grandchildren made it, despite the snow, and a handful of people with some loose connection to Greta: neighbors, the mailman, a girl from Family Services . . . and, of course, Adeline Meier.

Adeline Meier, once a perky USO starlet, now a regular voice on KNUJ's morning obituary announcements and "Adeline's Eats" cooking show, attended every funeral in New Ulm. Sending off the dead with a peck on the cheek and a snappy tune was her calling, she said. Bereaved families didn't care much for Adeline's rendition of "God Bless America" sung over their loved ones, but this was rural Minnesota—no one wanted to be rude and tell her to leave. They sat and smiled, nodded their thanks, and grumbled about her behind her back. Everyone knew that Adeline not only went through the funeral lunch lines twice, she also brought Tupperware containers in her tote bag to stock up on thirds and fourths, packing them tight with ham, potato salad, and frosted brownies.

"God has called his daughter Greta home," Father Schmalfeld began, following the opening hymn. "Let us be happy for her, knowing she has found eternal peace in His kingdom."

The tiny group mumbled "Amen" in unison and settled back into their folding chairs.

Frieda's funeral had been beautiful, held on a warm, fresh morning in May, 1968, the smell of roses and orchids swirling from the open doors of St. Mary's. The large church filled quickly with hundreds of people to whom Frieda's death—a heart attack in her sleep— was an unexpected blow. During the visitation, Greta refused to stand in the receiving line, sitting instead on a metal chair in the far corner of the room, partially hidden behind a grouping of umbrella trees. At the funeral the next day, she sat and stood alone, off to the side, wide-brimmed black hat dipped low, as friends and family, including Eleanor, retold old stories about Frieda's quick wit, good heart, and heavenly recipes for German potato salad and *Lebkuchen*. Greta said nothing. And despite the large number of people in attendance, no one sandwiched inside those pews knew how broken apart Frieda's little sister Greta was inside. They didn't know there'd be no fixing her.

"At this time," Father Schmalfeld said, "I'd like to invite you all to share a story about Greta with the rest of us. Perhaps a remembrance that best highlights why she was so loved."

The furnace blower kicked, and the flames of the candelabra spooked.

Ana Zins, from Ana's Saloon, rocked herself out of her chair in the front row and turned to face the congregation. She folded her arms beneath her breasts, her left hand slowly rubbing her right forearm.

"I just had a little something to say. Nothing much." She spoke to her empty chair. "'Cept that Greta first come into the joint about, oh, 30-some years ago now. I remember this one time, October, I think, she comes in all shook up and says, 'Shit, Ana, I hit a deer this morning.'"

Father Schmalfeld inhaled and held the breath high in his chest, lips pursed, no doubt anticipating additional verbal punches as Ana continued her story.

"And I says, 'You hit a deer?' And she says, '*Ja*, with the Ford. Well, I didn't really hit it,' she says, 'I bumped it.'

"'You bumped it?'

"'*Ja*, I bumped it.'

"'Where?'

"'Back legs.'

"'Ach,' I says, '*where were you* when you hit it?'

"'Well, that's the thing. I was going uphill.'

"'What?'

"'Up toward Flandrau, there. Deer was just standing in the middle of the road. Just standing. And I seen it too late and bumped it. Then the damn thing shook its head at me and pissed on the hood.'"

Ana giggled and wiped a finger below her nose. "I just thought that was kinda funny," she said, turning toward Father Schmalfeld. "I think she totaled that car the next year. Grill looked like it'd been upholstered. That was something to see, boy. Deer hair sticking out everywhere. Ach, *so was . . .* "

People chuckled, and Ana turned around and fell back into her seat.

Programs rustled. Throats were cleared. Someone in back wheezed. Eleanor looked to her left and saw a young mother of two she didn't know elbow her older boy. He stood up wearing an oversized Minnesota Vikings jacket, his hands pulled tight inside the sleeves, his cheeks ripe and full as pomegranates—rare fruit in corn country.

"Um, yeah," he began. "Me and my mom used to do Meals on Wheels for . . . um . . . "

He hesitated—and he did so, Eleanor knew, because he was unsure of what to call that woman lying in front. He didn't know her name, first or last, just that her house was dark inside and small. Magazine clippings, receipts, newspapers, and coupons covered the floor, as if a majestic paper tree had once towered over the house and then let go of its leaves one clear fall day. A TV no bigger than the boy's lunchbox skipped and rolled its programs green. When the boy set the hot meal down on the counter, a black dog struggled to its feet and lumbered onto the linoleum with slow clicks. Plates and bowls filled the double sink. The old lady always wore a shapeless dress, like the gown the boy's mother had probably worn at the hospital when she delivered his little brother. And the hair on the old lady's head, lint gray, always looked as though it was trying to fly far away. She rattled on and on about bad eyes, Dan Rather, the boy's sweet cheeks, and what a bastard the Lord God was.

Mostly, though, the boy knew that she always smelled like pee, warm pee. He, and everyone else in town, knew Eleanor's sister Greta as The Pee Lady.

That was the story every person in the funeral home knew but wouldn't say, how every day during the last few years Greta had shuffled north along Minnesota Street, past the Chamber of Commerce and Reichman's Books, two knick-knack stores and seven bars, a bank, and a coffee shop, to the glockenspiel and the buzzing ball of tourists that bounced around the tower at 1:00 and 3:00, heads thrown back, mouths open, ready to receive the spinning statues and German bells like communion wafers. At the glockenspiel, she turned west, up a block to Broadway, the main drag through town, and shuffled back south past Henle's Funeral Home, the police and fire stations, Ana's Saloon, the public library, and the Red Owl. Wearing a cotton housedress, scuffs, and no underwear, Greta relieved herself whenever she had need. Sometimes on the grass. More often the sidewalks and curbs. Parking lots. Along lunch counters and store aisles. Ana Zins was one of just a handful who kept their doors open to Greta. Most places watched for her and escorted her out, kept someone at the door during the busy tourist season to make sure she didn't slip in and turn customers away with her sharp smell and Biblical rantings. The coffee shop owner, tired finally of mopping and disinfecting the booth after Greta's visits, tired of listening to his employees bribe each other with shifts so they wouldn't have to wait on her, told Greta she should seek some medical attention, that he was sorry but she wasn't welcome in his shop anymore.

Eleanor heard the stories whispered about her sister between pews at church, over tables at the senior center, and from the mouths of friends who'd been shopping downtown. Her husband brought home talk from his daily coffee circle at McDonald's. Just as often, though, Eleanor heard stories from Greta herself during their weekly calls—complaints about the rudeness and intolerance of people these days, her mistreatment at the hands of so many hypocritical "good Christians," how a person had to walk a mile for one friendly word, and what the hell kind of world did we live in anyway?

The boy in the Vikings jacket continued to struggle. "We, um, did Meals on Wheels for, um . . . " He pointed to Greta's casket. "For *her*. And this one time, I went in, and she said she had something for me. And, um, she gave me an ice-cream pail with snowmen on it and stuff. And she said I could use it to put my pencils in." The boy stopped, pleased with himself for having gotten this far. "Mom had to wash it when we got home, 'cause there was still some old ice cream in it."

His mother tugged gently on his jacket.

"But then she had to throw it away," the boy continued, "'cause she said she couldn't get the smell out."

At that, the mother yanked her son down onto his chair, quickly looked at the other people in the room with a nervous smile, and patted her son's sleeve.

Eleanor expected that to be the end. And it was. No one else had anything to say. Eighty years on this earth reduced to a couple dozen mourners, a story about dead deer, and a plastic pail laced with rancid ice cream.

Father Schmalfeld raised his eyebrows expectantly and scanned the room, then half-smiled, nodded, and told everyone to bow their heads to pray. He blessed Greta's soul, offered prayers for those inside and outside the walls of the funeral home, extended his condolences to Eleanor, and told the congregation that the family invited them all to a little lunch over at the Legion following the closing hymn. With the weather being so bad, he added, people needn't follow out to the cemetery but please, go right over for some tater-tot hotdish.

The organist tripped through her elaborate introduction, and everyone stood and sang.

When the service was over, Ray went outside to warm up the car, bring it around to the door. People told Eleanor they'd see her at the Legion, so they could chat a bit. The organist, already wrapped tight inside her wool coat and scarf, thanked Eleanor for the lunch invitation but said the snow was piling up, she lived over near Courtland, and that 14 was a bitch of a road with the drifting. Eleanor told her to drive safe.

Before the funeral director closed the casket, Eleanor patted her sister's hands, touched the black beads now wrapped around those waxen fingers. Eleanor thought Greta might need the rosary, a little insurance policy for her once she crossed over. She looked at Greta's face and saw in that strong nose their mother, their sister Frieda, all the children and grandchildren. There was no hiding the family resemblance. Not with hair, hats, or a heart attack.

But Eleanor recognized nothing else. With the heat of her anger gone, Greta's face had blossomed, opened pink and petal-smooth. Her hair lay quiet as cirrus clouds across her blue, cotton shoulders, while the air trumpeted lilies and pine.

Ray fought to close the door behind him and stomped the snow from his boots. "Ready, Norrie?"

Eleanor nodded and closed the top button of her coat.

As the director prepared to remove the casket, Adeline Meier rose from her chair and placed her right hand over her heart. A small American flag waved from her lapel. She opened her mouth to sing.

Ray held the door for his wife, put a hand out to steady her, said that even if Adeline didn't sing all the verses, the snow was sure to slow her down considerably, enough so that they might even get seconds of the ambrosia before Adeline got her firsts. Eleanor stepped out, raised her chin high, and let winter bless every last inch of her face.

SCHULTZ

S OME MEN KNOW CARS. Others know football, baseball, what type of bait is sure to snag a pan-size walleye. Marty Schultz knew fire. Even though he'd never been a fireman himself, he knew all the volunteers in town and who their folks had been, who was always first on a call, what equipment they used, how many elevators, barns, and trailers had been eaten by fire in Brown County over the past 12 months, and, of course, who torched them. He gleaned nuggets of information from his police scanner at home or a few well-placed calls to retired firemen, and he delighted in sharing the news with the other old regulars at Ana's Saloon.

"Say," Marty said, hoisting himself onto a red vinyl stool, "hear about Fisher's boy?"

Ana hooked a bottle of Schell's under the edge of the counter for him, snapped off the cap. Marty was always her first customer of the day, smart in his pressed, blue Dickies. Ana shook her head and wiped her hands on her apron. "Set another one?"

"Mmm-hmm. Lit his wife's car up like a bonfire last night. One of them Mazel Tov cocktails right through the window. 'Course they ain't got no proof yet that it's him." Marty took a swallow. "Thinks she's getting more than ground beef and brats from City Meats, if you know what I mean. Figures that butcher, George Roiger's kid, Brian, is slipping her the 'sausage special.'"

Ana turned the volume down on the TV and up on the radio. Mid-morning meant KNUJ's regional obituaries, followed by a 15-minute cooking show. Today's topic was Holiday Hotdishes.

"I'd like to make something special for the Christmas Eve party tomorrow," Ana said. "I found a recipe for lime-flavored Knox Blox. I bet a guy could use a cookie cutter to cut 'em into Christmas trees instead of squares. Something kind of different."

Marty rustled through the morning papers and hummed.

Ana grabbed a couple lemons from a wire basket on the back bar. "And it's 'Molotov,' not 'Mazel Tov.'"

"Whatever," Marty mumbled.

The saloon brightened as Ana sliced neat wedges and wheels for the garnish caddy. "*Ja*, I heard the sirens last night around—ach—couldn't have been earlier than midnight, I guess. 1:00?"

"Me and you did the right thing, Ana," Marty said, scanning football stats. "Didn't get mixed up in that whole marriage business. Think of all the messes we saved ourselves from, boy . . . I tell you."

The radio woman rattled off a list of people who had passed away in the last day or two, visitation hours, and where the burial was, in the same carnival-barker way she announced meat specials at the local grocer: "Alphonse BUSHARD, NINE—ty-TWO, DIED last night at LORETTA HOSPITAL. He's surVIVED by his wife, MARY, TEN GRANDchildren, and many GREAT-grandchildren. PICK UP a POUND of GROUND CHUCK, NINE—ty cents this week only at your NEIGH—borhood RED OWL store. The STORE—for value."

"This weather," Ana began, "honest to God, it's killing people left and right. It's getting so a guy doesn't know who's dead and who you just haven't seen in a while."

Just then, the radio burst into "The Liechten-steiner Polka," signaling the start of "Adeline's Eats." The radio woman, Adeline Meier, now finished with her list of the dead, barked her way through three holiday hotdish recipes. The polka looped continuously in the background.

"She sure knows how to get people's attention," Ana said. "I'll give her that. We went to school together, you know. Up at Trinity. She was our class valedictorian."

"TWO—cans cream of MUSH—room SOUP, and TWO—cans PEAS."

Ana tapped her pencil to the bouncy music and scribbled part of a recipe in between measures. "She was a smart one, but kinda loose, too."

The bell over the front door jingled. Two other regulars shuffled in, shoulders hunched from the cold, and settled onto the stools next to Marty. Ana smiled and slid two beers and the stack of papers over to them. When KNUJ's "Farmers' Market Report" began, Ana walked back to the grill, one hand steadying her along the wall.

"So. Fisher the Firestarter's at it again, huh?" one of the men asked, wiping the ice from his beard. "He's a crazy one, that Fisher."

"He's just looking for attention," Marty said.

Pots and pans clanged together in the back room. Cupboards and the refrigerator door thudded repeatedly. Ana flipped the exhaust fan switch. The blades spun like old bomber propellers.

"Well, maybe he ought'a do something *deserving* of attention, then," the second man said, thumbing slowly through the newspaper sections. "Something decent, like joining the Army, saving the country from Communists. Not this arson shit. Even if she *is* futzing around. Christ."

Marty stood up, pulled a couple bills from his wallet, tossed them onto the wood.

"George's boy sure as hell better watch his back," the second man continued, "that's all I gotta say. Crazy fucker's liable to go after him next, set the whole goddamn butcher shop on fire."

His coat buttoned, Marty tied down the earflaps on his cap, pushed his hands deep into his pockets. He felt chilled, despite all the talk of fire.

"Hey! Marty!" Ana yelled from the grill, waving her hand. "Come here! I gotta ask you something!"

Marty walked back into the cloud of grease.

"Say, you wanna be Santa again this year?" Ana stabbed at each piece of bacon in the skillet and turned it over. "I couldn't pay you nothing, you know that, but the kids should have a Santa to hand out presents and stuff. I still got the costume up in the attic." She looked up at the tin ceiling and pointed at it with her fork. "I just hope those squirrels didn't make some kind of nest or something in it. Remember I had those squirrels up there? *Gott im Himmel.*"

"That'd be fine," Marty answered. He flipped up his coat collar and pulled it tight around his throat. "I'm gonna head down to George's, then. See you tomorrow."

George's Ballroom was as much a part of Marty as his old bones. It warmed his blood and felt like home. Its neon face and smoky voice had teased him since 1948, when he had slow-danced with his first love, Agnes Brandel, out on its shiny wooden floor.

The Brandels had farmed a few miles outside town, out near Klossner, a blink of a village with a post office and grain elevator on one side of the road and a bar sticky with disappointment on the other. Brandels' place was a modest set-up: a small coop of chickens, a few horses and cows, couple dogs, cats, and a house stuffed to the beams with children. Marty had always felt a connection with Agnes, even though he'd been a townie himself. Whenever the other kids in class had refused to sit by her because she smelled of horse, Marty had slid his chair close, shared the jelly sandwich his mother had packed for him, and kept Agnes from tears.

The day he had asked her to the Valentine's Day dance at George's Ballroom, she had paled, her eyes wide and wild. He'd seen that look before on his uncle's cows, when the dogs danced too tight around their legs. She stammered something about chores and having nothing nice enough to wear, and then bolted down the front steps of the school, leaving behind a trail of pencils and bread crust. Although he was only 14 years old and didn't know much of anything about girls, Marty understood that her answer was a firm "no."

But that night, as he sat along the edge of the dance floor with the other boys, staring across the abyss at the girls, chaperones swimming from side to side trying desperately to bring the two groups together, in walked Agnes Brandel and her older brother, Frank.

Marty would later claim that all the other children dissipated like steam when her curled red hair, pulled back by a blue bow, charged the air in the room. She wore a blue-and-white-checkered cotton dress beneath her wool coat, knee-high boots with a narrow fur fringe, the pair she most likely wore only to Sunday church. Her brother swung her black shoes—their laces tied to one another—by his little finger. Some of the girls snickered, whispered not so quietly about how old Agnes' dress was and how many times they'd seen her wear it. But Marty didn't see the frayed hem, faded color, or how her sleeves stopped short halfway between her wrists and elbows. To him, Agnes was an enchanting blue flame.

She scanned the room, and Marty tried to catch her eye with a little wave. Frank chucked his sister lightly on the shoulder and then headed over to the bar. Marty could feel the panic rise from the soles of Agnes' feet, climb up her neck, flushing her cheeks and making her eyes water. He half-walked, half-ran over to her, afraid she'd bolt again if he didn't act quickly.

"Hey," Marty said. "Didn't think you was coming. Sure glad you did, though. You look real nice."

Agnes didn't say anything, and the space between them grew thick.

Marty scratched the back of his neck and cleared his throat once, then again. "Got a haircut a couple days ago, and it's already growing back itchy," he laughed. "Yours probably don't do that, though, huh? For girls it's probably different."

Agnes, who'd been staring at the middle of Marty's chest as he spoke, finally looked up into his face and bit her lower lip. Marty knew if she cried, it'd be all over, so he reached for her hands.

"Hey, c'mon," he said just under his breath. "Tell you what. Just stay for a little while. Just try it. And then if you still hate it and wanna leave, I'll walk you out, okay?"

"Okay," Agnes said.

So they stood alongside each other for a long time, glasses of punch cupped in their hands, watching couples slowly venture out into the deep water, chaperones encouraging them in their wake. Eventually Marty and Agnes were swept into the current themselves, and they danced, hesitant at first, but that space between them turning finally fluid and easy. They swayed and spun, hopped and kicked until the band folded its music, pulled its instruments apart, and tucked them back into their cases. Marty held Agnes' coat while she reached back and slid her arms into the sleeves. And Agnes, her eyes sharp and clear, smiled.

Once outside, Agnes said she'd had a nice time after all, that she'd see him Monday at school. Marty wanted to bottle the frozen breath that puffed out between her lips with each word, save it for summer days when the sun burned and blistered. Frank, again carrying Agnes' shoes on his little finger, whistled his sister over to an idling truck parked across the street.

Marty wanted to tell Agnes how he loved the smell of hay and horse in her hair and would watch out for her for the rest of her life if she'd let him. Instead he blurted, "Wanna go see the fire trucks?"

"What?" Agnes asked.

"The fire trucks. My pa's a fireman. He's over at the station. Just thought if you ain't never been on a fire truck before, maybe you might wanna—I don't know—get on one. Tonight."

Agnes hesitated. Frank whistled again. "But my brother's driving me home. I live—"

"Pa can drive you home later. He wouldn't mind. Klossner ain't that far."

"C'mon, Aggie! Let's go!" Frank yelled.

Agnes wiped her mitten beneath her nose, cocked her head, and sighed. "Oh, just a minute," she said, and then ran across the street. Her arms swung back and forth in large arcs as she ran, and

Marty believed that she actually took flight, lifted off the ground, her red curls suspended in the air.

He didn't hold her hand as they walked the two blocks to the fire station. Something inside him warned that he might spoil everything if he pushed his luck, so he was content to walk alongside, occasionally bumping shoulders. He smiled as she stepped up on the running board of Pumper Number 1 and then sat tall in the driver's seat while he imitated a siren wail. He laughed as she squealed her way down the pole from the sleeping quarters upstairs, her knuckles white and a bright spark in her eyes. And he felt a small fire warm his heart when she cocked the metal helmet on her head and turned to look at herself in the mirror, the name "Schultz" in yellow letters painted on the back of her crown.

The old building didn't just conjure up memories of Agnes. George's Ballroom also fed Marty his first mixed drink and cigar (and nursed his first hangover), whispered to him about the trouble smoldering in Korea. Marty wanted to be a pilot, making bombing runs over railroads, bridges, and bunkers. He outlined in detail the advantages of the Sabre over the Soviets' MiG-15 to the old men at the bar and was quick to heat up when anyone disagreed with him. He drew maps on cocktail napkins, tracked Kim Il Sung's push into Seoul, and marked bases with big black stars where local boys were supposedly already stationed. He dreamed of returning to New Ulm a hero, his John Wayne bravery pinned to his chest, beneath confetti-filled skies, trumpet blasts and snare drums echoing off the storefront brick along Minnesota Street.

But it wasn't to be. And it was George's Ballroom that took a beating from Marty, the broken glass and hole in the wall, when he found out the Army hadn't accepted him on account of his widowed mother. It was the Ballroom, too, that held him close when the names of his friends killed in action lodged in his throat and made him gag. It was the Ballroom that bought him another drink and another and another when Agnes Brandel slipped and suffocated in her family's grain silo. No other place knew his name so well or understood what it all meant to be Marty Schultz, the curly-haired kid who'd never left his hometown, never married, spent his whole life sweeping up after other people, cleaning tables, folding and unfolding chairs.

"If you could get here around 8:00 tomorrow morning, that should give us plenty of time to set up," George Roiger said, restocking the waitress station. "Buffet won't start till 6:00, cocktails at 5:00. You're coming back down for supper, right, Marty?"

Marty nodded and looked back at the wet trail of snow he'd tracked in with his boots. He'd have to remember to lay down extra mats by the doors tomorrow. More snow was on the way. The last thing he needed was to have some woman in her Christmas heels flying through the air.

"I told Ana I'd be Santa again for the party at the joint tomorrow, but that shouldn't be a problem. I got the timing all worked out."

"Good. Brian got in some of the finest sirloin in the area. Same distributor as those fancy places up in the Cities. Nothing but the best for my customers." George popped a cherry in his mouth and smiled. "I got a tradition to live up to here, you know. Want to have something respectable to pass on to the kid when I retire."

Marty raised his hand to say good-bye and followed the widening trail of melted snow out the door. He lived just six blocks from George's, four from the fire station, three from Ana's Saloon. It wasn't a long walk, except on days like this, when the wind slapped his face with an open palm, leaving its mark on his cheeks—a sting so cold, it felt hot. Nothing good ever came from weather like this.

Late that night, Marty woke, panting, his sheets soaked through. He stumbled to the window, cranked it open, and let the sub-zero air swirl around and between his legs, across his chest. There was smoke somewhere near. Smoke, and a hot, wicked flame.

Marty stuck his head outside. All lay quiet and still. Tame smoke from neighborhood chimneys rose straight up into the clear, star-filled sky.

Moments later, sirens cried like wolves, headed down into the valley in packs. The rumble of Engine 1, 3, and the Hook vibrated though Marty's nightstand and rattled his lamp. He closed his eyes and stood in front of the open window, listened to the straining police car engines, the rude blast of the pumper horn, and the sharp wrench of a missed gear. Just blocks for the trucks to go, but help would be too late. Marty could feel it inside him. Tonight's was a mean, unforgiving fire. And not the butcher shop. Far, far worse.

After a few minutes, Marty shut the window and crawled back into bed. He knew he could sleep in tomorrow. George wouldn't mind or even notice. He'd have other things to do.

"I hung the costume up in back. Cleaned up good," Ana said. She set her party favor bags out on the card table. "One of those squirrels was on it after all, all stiff and dead, but it didn't seem to hurt the suit. I think it was because it was so cold up there, you know, that it didn't smell or decay or something."

Marty nodded and shuffled back behind the grill, taking the suit into the restroom.

The saloon had been transformed overnight into a winter wonderland, complete with evergreen garlands, "Merry Xmas" scrawled in red lipstick across the mirror over the back bar, a string of blinking white lights tacked over the doorway, and plastic poinsettias on each table. Kettles bubbled with sauerkraut and dumplings, boiled *Landejägers*, and homemade *Spätzle*. The smell of warm pork meatloaf and rye loaves hung from the ceiling. Small green gelatin trees quivered on a plastic tray shaped like a snowman head.

The regulars arrived with their children and grandchildren around 4:00, bright in their new Christmas sweaters. Marty waited back by the grill for Ana's signal. The suit had shrunk from last year. The hem of the pants just touched the elastic of his black socks. No doubt Ana had thrown it in a hot dryer, just to make sure it would be ready in time for the party. The felt rim of the hat made his scalp itch.

The radio had told him over breakfast what he'd already known about last night's fire. For Marty, the flames had taken more than George's walls. It had swallowed a country girl's blue-and-white-checkered dress whole. Marty had smelled her scorched hair and the charred dance floor from his bedroom window. Glass had popped behind the bar and dripped in the back offices. The color and feel of the ceiling and walls had been licked clean by the fire's tongue. Soot had fallen like a bad snow, drifted deep between the burned tables and chairs and within the firemen's lungs. Hisses of steam. Crackling wood. The black collapse of roof beams. From miles away, folks up for a late-night snack said it looked like New Ulm had grown an angry orange blister.

Without George's, Marty didn't know who he was. The mirror behind the bar there had always told him: high-school boy in love, grieving son, angry teenager, disappointed bachelor, reliable maintenance man. He had stored his memories in the ballroom's closets, taped them underneath the countertops, and looped them around the brass railings and the long, gold arms of the chandeliers.

He couldn't play Santa. Not today. He had to go home. But before he could turn and head out the back door of the saloon, fall back three blocks to the safety of his darkened bungalow, Ana pulled her earlobe—the signal. He quickly wiped his eyes, rifled through a drawer, and found a pair of large, round sunglasses. He put them on and hoisted the brown lawn-and-leaf bag filled with gifts over his shoulder. Ana set the needle on her first 45 of the evening—"Jingle Bell Rock"—and Marty walked out ho-ho-ho-ing.

"Look! It's Santa!" Ana cried, her hands outstretched. "Santa! Merry Christmas, Santa!"

One by one Marty set the kids on his knee, listened to their wishes, and explained away his sunglasses with talk of "terrible snow blindness." Some cried, a few didn't say anything, unsure what to think about a Santa wearing shades and tennis shoes. Marty hugged each one of them and passed out gifts until his bag was empty.

After the last little boy waved good-bye and the bell over the front door jingled for the last time, Marty sat down in a booth, took off his hat and sunglasses, ground the heels of his hands into his tired eyes. He knew he'd been flying too low for too long but couldn't see for the smoke. He wasn't safe. If he didn't pull up soon, he'd lose it all in the trees.

"You're still here," Ana said, shuffling in from the grill area. "I thought you'd gone home already."

Marty shook his head. "Thought I'd see if there was anything else you needed help with."

Ana set two open beer bottles at Marty's booth and rolled her wide hips onto the bench seat across from him. She nudged one of the bottles to his hand. "Merry Christmas. Don't say I never gave you nothing." She smiled and scratched the top of her forearm.

"And I didn't get you nothing," Marty said. He reached over to the next table, grabbed a white plastic poinsettia, and chuckled. "Here."

Ana thanked him and tucked it behind her ear.

The TV was still on, mute, an episode of "The Mary Tyler Moore Show" playing in black and white. Christmas music by the Ray Conniff Singers slow-danced across the empty bar, the neon Schell's and Grain Belt signs lighting the polished wood.

"Sorry about George's, there," Ana said. "Honest to God, I don't know how someone could do that. On Christmas, too." She ran her thumb around the mouth of her bottle. "Makes a guy just sick."

Marty tightened a few strands of silver tinsel around his little finger. Ana leaned back in the booth, her arms folded, rubbing her elbows.

"How'd you ever make out with that stuff from the doctor?" Marty asked.

"For my psoriasis, you mean?" Ana clucked her tongue. "*Ja*, they wanted $30 for a little tube-like thing of this 'medicated cream.' Had some stuff in there I didn't know what it was. That lotion I sent for off the TV only cost $19.95, and you get twice as much! All natural, too. Go figure." She took a long swallow. Then another. "It helps a little bit. Can't complain too much, I guess."

She sighed and looked out the window, scraped frost off the glass with her fingernail.

"Say, Marty," she said, "you ever think much about your pa? I mean, did you ever wonder how your life would've been different if he hadn't of died so young? I think about that with my pa. And Johnny. Especially this time of year."

Marty cleared his throat and took a swig, wet his lips. "I didn't really know him," he said. "He was always working, you know, out at the brewery, down at the fire station. Everybody thought he was decent, though. Good fireman. I know that much."

Ana finished her beer. "I like to think they're all watching out for me up there. Ma, too." She turned her sunglasses over in her hands. "Looking down from Heaven and making sure I'm all right."

The cuckoo clock behind the bar sang 10:00. The nightly civil defense whistle blew a minute later. Marty and Ana watched the quiet TV for a few minutes without a word.

"I don't know what all my dad thought of me," Marty said eventually. "He never told me, see. And, well, then he died." He closed his eyes, felt a draft nip at his ankles. "Don't know if I was what he wanted or not. But . . . shouldn't matter now anyhow, right?" He chuckled under his breath.

The radio station was breaking up. Static crackled inside Nat King Cole's throat.

"Let me get you another beer," Ana said. She slid across the bench seat and pushed herself up with a grunt, one hand on the table, the other gripping the side of the booth.

Marty slid out, too, and picked up his bag of clothes and leftovers. "That's okay, Ana. I should get going anyways. Been a hell of a long day."

"You sure? I can get you another one."

Marty shook his head.

Ana scratched her elbow and shifted her weight from one leg to the other. "It has been one hell of a day, boy," she said. "Well, Merry Christmas, then." She put her hands on Marty's shoulders, pulled him down to her, and kissed him on the cheek. "God bless. You take care now."

Marty nodded and walked to the door. He looked through the window, across the street to the fire station, its sickly evergreen lit with faded blue bulbs. Time for the city to buy some new strings, he thought. Multicolor would be nice. Transplant a new tree. A sturdy one to hold the heavy, wet snow.

He turned around, and Ana was still standing there, small, the high tin ceiling above her, white poinsettia behind her ear.

"Say, I was thinking," Marty began, looking down at his shoes. "I don't really got to go home for nothing special, you know, so, since it's Christmas and all, maybe I should just stay here awhile yet and keep you company. So's you weren't all alone. It'd sorta be my Christmas present to you." He cleared his throat. "Okay?"

Ana smiled and took a deep breath. She nodded, slowly walked side-to-side toward the bar. Marty set down his bag and hoisted himself onto a red vinyl stool.

He knew he still had a long way to go—you didn't undo years' worth of damage in a couple hours—but sitting there in the saloon with Ana, he heard his father shout and give the "All Clear" deep inside his heart. Marty would go in tomorrow morning, salvage what he could from the steaming mess, and slowly begin to build again.

BLUE SNOW

*M*OLLY SCHUH KNEW she had an odd heart. She'd never seen it, of course, but she'd heard it, felt it flutter beneath her palm with its strong, gray wings. It was a willful heart, powerful enough to lift her right off her feet. Didn't matter if she was playing Wiffleball in gym class or fingering scales on her clarinet. When her heart beat its wings, up Molly rose. The fact was, Molly's heart did what it pleased. It simply would not be told what to do.

But Molly had a plan to clip her heart's wings, to show it who was boss. Day after day, she ate as much as she could stomach—cookies and cupcakes, third helpings at dinner, boxes of sugary cereal, chocolate and ice cream—in hopes of weighting herself down, becoming too much for her heart to lift. At night, she made her mother tuck the sheets in tight to her throat and fell asleep gripping the edge of the mattress, just in case her heart had a mind to take flight while she was dreaming.

Two summers ago, down at the German Park pool, Molly felt her special heart for the first time. Her best friend, Piper, had crawled across the deep end, waved, and shouted to Molly, who was still standing knee-deep in "Little Kids' Lagoon," an inflatable ring wedged around her waist.

"I am *not* a baby!" Molly yelled back, wriggling out of the ring and tossing it onto the deck. She sloshed toward the far end of the pool until the water licked her chin, keeping her eyes on Piper and the black "5 ft." mark behind Piper's head. She cupped her hands and made small scooping motions. Her feet bounced off the pool bottom, started to flip back and forth like clumsy fins. "See? I can *too* swim!" she shouted above the splash.

Midway across, though, her arms tired, and the sides of her body pinched. She gulped water and went under.

The green water wrapped itself around her like a warm cotton blanket. Suspended, her hands reaching for a sun that rippled and furled, Molly felt safe, as though it were natural that she should be there, weightless, caught between the surface and the hard, blue floor—everything reduced to an odd gurgle.

Then she felt the muscles in her heart's wings flex and catch air.

"Molly Ann, what were you thinking?" Mrs. Schuh asked as soon as they got home from the pool. "Trying to go all the way across . . . Piper's a better swimmer than you. Thank goodness that lifeguard was watching." She looked at her daughter, wrapped from neck to knees in a wet beach towel, and shook her head. "I can't believe you did something so stupid. Now go take off that suit. And be sure to rinse out the chlorine."

Molly lay in bed that night replaying the hour at the pool over and over in her head—the chlorine sting in the back of her throat, the long string of bubbles pulled from her nose and mouth, how she had hung between one world and another. She'd panicked. Pure instinct. That's what had happened. The adrenaline had flushed her heart out from behind her ribs, awakened it from a long sleep. Like a spooked pheasant her heart had lit, wings fully extended, sharp as fresh-cut paper. It had thrashed inside, confused, knocking against bone and tissue, until it had found its rhythm, righted itself, and carried Molly to the water's surface.

If she had just stayed calm, things would have been okay. She pulled the covers to her chin and tried to breathe quietly, listening for the slightest rustle, one vibrating quill. Hot tears pooled in her ears. She closed her eyes and hoped her heart wouldn't do that again.

But it would.

The Schuhs' refrigerator was buried beneath drawings Molly had made of herself and her pet rabbit, Charlotte. In each, Molly's heart, a red smudge with thick, bowed lines growing out each side, pulsed far bigger and brighter than the sun and its spiky yellow rays. Mrs. Schuh taped each picture to the fridge, touched the crayon hearts, and smiled.

"Honey, that's so sweet, you wanting to be a flight attendant and all." She ran her finger along the gray curves. "Look here, you've got your little airplane wings, too, those pins with the wings, just like the real thing."

"No, Mom, that's my *heart*. I told you. Remember?"

Mrs. Schuh opened the fridge and grabbed a carton of eggs. "But, Molly, I'll tell you what. You can't be any kind of flight attendant looking like you do now." She cracked an egg on the edge of the mixing bowl and rolled the yolk back and forth inside the shell halves, separating it from the white. "You can't be fat if you're going to work in an airplane. You'd never fit through those tiny aisles."

Molly stuffed a brownie square in her mouth, pulled on, zipped, and buttoned her winter clothes, then headed outside to feed her rabbit.

Charlotte was Molly's best friend now. Molly's talk of having a heart with wings—and her frequent fainting spells—had turned Molly into a target at school, and all her old friends, including Piper, had decided it was better to leave her to the wolves than risk being branded "friend to the freak." Molly didn't blame her friends for running away. She would run away from herself, too, if she could.

Sleet spit against the windows. Charlotte wasn't waiting outside her box today. She huddled in the back corner, shivering.

Molly unlocked the top of the cage and lifted the roof off Charlotte's box. She reached in and slid her mittened hand beneath the rabbit's belly, cupping it like a bubble. "C'mon, you. Aren't you hungry or what?" She cocked her elbow and turned the rabbit's nose to hers. "Wake up, you big sleepy—"

Molly stopped.

Charlotte's eyes stared wide, cold, ears flat back, the fur covering her face stiff with dried blood. A pink spot the size of a pencil eraser glistened where her nose should have been.

Molly's mouth opened. Her eyes blurred. She felt the frantic beat of the rabbit's heart through the layers of woven cotton. It ran down her arm, through the twists of nerves that filled her body, and dared her own heart to follow. And Molly's heart, answering to no one, especially not Molly, did just that.

"No," Molly whimpered, "not again. You just be still."

In an instant, her heart was off. It slipped past tree trunks and grazed low wire. It skirted snake holes, squeezed through rotted barn doors, hugged the earth in a full-out run until it finally knocked beat for beat with the cottontail's well-oiled heart.

The wind shrieked, and Molly smelled the cat behind her, heard its rhythmic puffs of air. She couldn't remember how to say her own name, couldn't make her lips wrap around the consonants. Faster and faster the hearts raced. She felt as though with each full extension she was rising above herself, watching her body struggle to stay ahead in the chase. Farther and farther up she rose until the day turned colder and the moon slipped over the horizon. Up over the dark pine tips, until she could no longer hear the controlled breath of the cat or smell the blood on its rough tongue. Up until her body was nothing more than a black dot darting across a field of blue snow.

Molly feared it was only a matter of time before the snow piled so dark there would be no distinction between black and blue, between those things that moved and those that didn't, that she'd float so far she'd never come back down.

Last December, Molly had gotten stuck deep inside a network of tunnels the neighborhood boys had carved into the 15-foot drifts along the road.

"Hey! Lard-ass!" they called. "Dare you to crawl through our Tunnel of Death!"

Molly looped the pull rope on her red plastic sled around her hand and dragged it over to the boys.

They stood in front of the tunnel, arms hugging their chests. Molly wiped her nose with the back of her mitten.

"We'll let you use our runner sled," the oldest one said. The others nodded and smiled.

"Yeah," another piped up, "we'll walk with you over to Westside Hill for some *real* sledding."

Molly looked at the gaping hole in the drift, the boys, and then back at the hole. "Okay, but then you can't call me names anymore. Fair enough?"

The oldest boy nodded. Two behind him snickered.

Molly propped her sled against the drift, then got down on her hands and knees and crawled into the tunnel's mouth, her snowmobile suit shushing against the snow. She wriggled through on her stomach, arms straight out front, moving one side of her body, then the other, back and forth like a slow purple piston.

A moment later, the tunnel swallowed her whole.

Snow pressed in on her hood, her shoulders, and hips. She couldn't move forward or backward. Loose flakes fell from the tunnel roof, hung on her eyelashes, and melted on the tip of her nose. She held her breath and listened. All around her the snow sighed.

Her heart ruffled its feathers, shook once inside her chest as though a blast of arctic air had cut it cleanly in two.

"Hey, guys?" she finally yelled. "Very funny. I'm stuck. I'm stuck! Get me out of here!" She called to the boys by name, at first good-hearted and hopeful, like she got the joke, then quickly turning scared as the boys continued to laugh and made no move to help her. "I'm telling on you guys! You're going to be in so much trouble! You're going to get it!"

She heard the muffled crunch of the boys' boots, the low groan of the snow beneath their weight. They pounded their fists on the tunnel walls in unison, chanting, "Molly, Molly's such a tard, looks just like a tub of lard. Eating this, eating that, man, that big ol' girl is fat!"

"C'mon, guys," Molly cried. "Please get me out of here. Please? I won't tell. I promise."

Molly listened for more laughter, but an odd quiet settled over the drift, leaving just the rapid thumping of her pulse in her ears. The boys had run off.

Light soon started to drain from the afternoon, and Molly knew the buried cornfields to the south of the tunnel were darkening and turning blue. Her nose dripped. She licked her upper lip. She heard her mother call her in for supper, twice, each syllable curling into the sky like chimney smoke. Molly had to pee so badly her belly hurt.

She didn't see any other way. The boys weren't coming back, and she'd never get out on her own. So she closed her eyes, took a deep breath, then whispered, "Okay. But just this once. And only because *I* say."

Molly knew it didn't matter what she said—she could've recited the Pledge of Allegiance; her heart would've paid the same heed—but she needed to feel as though she had *some* control over *something* in her small life. Short puffs of air caught in her throat, and she let out a cry. She thought she heard heavy footsteps, spaced far apart like her father's. She couldn't be sure. Her heart pounded hard inside its cage—strong, muscular beats from willful wings. Then all went black—and Molly slowly rose through the pile of snow.

She awoke on her back, near the rabbit cage, still clutching Charlotte with her mittened hands. A throbbing ache wrapped itself around her head like a wide bandage. The tree branches above her, the roofline of her parents' garage, and the clouds all melted together. She heard nothing except the whistle of the wind between the outbuildings and an open gate banging against its metal latch.

Molly pulled Charlotte tight to her chest, beneath her scarf, and wished she had brought the rabbit in the night before, when the cold front first iced the windows. She wished she could breathe in and out for two. Wished that the neighborhood cat had warmed its belly with a mouse instead of raking its claws across the cage wall and prizing Charlotte's nose. Looking up at the thick, gray sky, Molly wished she could stay grounded like the other kids and forget what it felt like to fly.

BENEATH MY SKIN
LIKE HONEY

*T*HE MOON ISN'T QUITE FULL, but it throws a wide sheet of light over the apartment building and tucks the ends in between each open blind and curtain. Peter and I are flying back to Minnesota in the morning, two days' worth of packing stacked along the walls like hay bales, things his mother, Ellie, left behind when her heart quit: afghans, doilies, iron pots and pans, house dresses and slippers that smell of cloves, a rubber-tipped cane, black-and-white photos curled in on themselves.

We made love on the trundle bed earlier tonight, after taping the last box made Peter cry. He didn't have anyone anymore, he said. No family. No reason ever to come back to New York. He slumped against the sofa and shook, chin to his chest. Not knowing what else to do, I hurried to the kitchen and poured him a glass of water. He watched me walk back into the room, his eyes wet and red, let me stroke his thinning hair until the dogs inside him heeled. He reached for me, locked his arms around my knees, and pulled me close. I cried, too—not because he'd lost his mother or his city, but because I knew in months I'd leave him so much more alone. That's just what my age would have me do.

Folding into and out of each other, we ticked off hours with the careful language our bodies spoke, one syllable at a time. The moon and streetlights smeared shadows across the walls, our faces, and backs. Gnarled trees branched into the ceiling, into the upstairs apartment, where I imagined the neighbor's mattress balanced in the limbs. The lines around Peter's eyes and mouth fell away in the dark. Sometime during the night, I swept them off the bed with the sheets.

We had been asleep for an hour or two when it woke me, this slow-breathing moon. Peter, sprawled on his stomach, one arm cocked over his head, swimming in some deep dream, made small sounds and twitched. I slipped to the window.

I never knew the moon made a sound, but it does. It's like Peter's breath in my ear, just before we've touched, that push of air through an open mouth, the kind that fogs the windows. And to learn it here, a most unlikely place, filled with late-night garbage trucks, subway thunder and squeal, sirens too wired to sleep.

If I say I *felt* the sound, felt it crawl just beneath my skin like honey, down my neck, the length of my arms, around each curve to the bottom of my feet, you'll think I'm trying too hard. But it is that way. Think about it. Fingernails on slate. The rumble of kettle drums. A voice pouring an aria into your ear.

Hearing is only part. We forget that sometimes. The truth is, we don't simply take in sounds and move on. We wince, shudder, stop breathing, set our jaws tight, or feel our cheeks flush the color of old barns and tractors.

Three months ago, back in Minnesota, a few miles outside the small town of New Ulm, Peter and I were walking the long gravel drive from his hobby farm to the highway, listening to the clicking and rattling of hard-shelled bugs in the corn, the shuffle of rabbit and fox. The clear, cool night was the first to break the July heat in weeks. A stray dog, the brown one with the broken leg, the one the neighbor backed over, hopped close behind us. Since the accident, whenever it heard a truck's gear drop into reverse, it howled and would not be quieted.

Nothing could hold the stars up that night. So many fell so fast we had to repeat the wishes we made on them—one wish for a dozen spots of light. It didn't matter, though. We didn't want much: Peter's mother to recover, the summer never to end, us to be together and to hell with the world. Once we reached the edge of the highway, Peter stopped. He tapped a cigarette, lit it, took a deep drag, and exhaled.

"So when Mother goes . . . ," he said, "whenever that is . . . would you fly out with me?" He talked down to the gravel, not much louder than a whisper.

"The arrangements, the packing . . . I should've been ready for this by now—Christ, she's 89—but I'm not. I'm really not."

He kicked a few stones with the toe of his boot, then turned back toward the farmhouse. With each step, he darkened a little more, until I lost him altogether, a seamless blend of denim and cornstalks, cotton and ditch weed.

I half-ran after him, the dog tight at my heels. It thought I was playing some sort of game and barked twice. The sound bounced off every grain elevator within miles and knocked more stars loose. When I reached Peter, we held each other, entwined like new lovers do, and the dog hobbled past on the trail of a coon.

We stood in the middle of the drive that way for a long time, through the hum of distant semis, hisses and wails of cats too far in heat, and a million bars of cicada song. When the odd dog hopped back out of the dark, nudged the bends of our legs, I told Peter I'd go along to New York, and we let the dog lead us home.

Ellie had lived here alone in this tiny apartment since 1961, the year Peter's father died, the year Ellie came home from grocery shopping and found her husband with half his skull blown away. It happened back there, in the bathroom. He finished a bottle of vodka, closed the door, and left without a note. The next day, the super started replacing the tile, painting the walls cornflower blue, the baseboards white, but there wasn't much he could do about the lingering gunpowder smell coiled behind every door, in every corner.

Ellie used to call Peter at all hours, crying, "I heard it. I heard it, Peter. That sound. And it's so awful. It's just . . . so, so awful."

This apartment doesn't frighten me, but there's an undeniable sadness soaked into these walls. I crack the window open, feel the cold run its tongue up the center of my body, and listen for something safe and familiar.

"Why don't you just go?" he said. "Get the hell out of here. You're going to leave me someday anyway." Peter poured himself another, swallowed it whole, and stared at me, his head hung low like a dazed bull. "Go on. Go on, little girl." He waved his hand toward the back door. "Your charity work for the old man is done. You passed with flying colors. Won't your mama be so proud?"

I walked out of the kitchen, settled into the living room couch, and opened my book. Doctors had given Ellie little more than a month to live at that point, they said her insides were softening, spoiling like fruit.

"I'm just like my dad, love," Peter called to me from the other side of the wall. "Bet you didn't know that." He snorted, then lowered his voice. "Yeah . . . he was a piece of work. Good ol' Kjell Bergqvist. Ha!" The sound of a screw cap being loosened. The pour. The bottle set heavy on the table. "Lost the family farm in Sweden. Moved his wife and son to New York. Then pissed away every dime he ever earned at any sorry-ass job he ever had." The scraping of chair legs on the kitchen floor. A stumble. A reeeeal winner." The click of a radio switch. Classical strings. "Mother was so happy when I moved out here with Jane . . . She liked her . . . She liked Mona and Kim, too." Louder violins and cellos. A soprano. The thud of the fridge door. Tin foil crackling. "A good life for me, that's all Mother ever wanted, God bless her."

Peter fell asleep at the kitchen table that night. In the morning, he apologized for words he couldn't remember, and I forgave him for being such a foolish old man.

"Remember that night we went out looking at stars?" I asked him, pouring water into the coffeemaker. "When we saw all of those stars falling at once?"

Peter folded back the front page of the newspaper. "End of July."

"Right," I said. "Well, I thought I actually *heard* a star fall. I didn't just *see* it, I *heard* it. I thought it made a noise." I pushed the brew button and set two mugs, spoons, and the sugar bowl on the table. "You were walking on ahead, and I just stood there, looking up at the sky, and I saw this streak of light and heard a mechanical kind of sound at the same time. I thought, wow, this is amazing." I dropped a couple frozen waffles in the toaster. "I mean, that had never happened before. Then I realized that I was still hearing the sound after the star had disappeared." The coffeemaker growled and dripped its last drop. "Thing is—well, that sound? It was actually Herm Engelmann's tractor. I could see the cab lights."

Peter looked at me over the top of his paper, his glasses near the tip of his nose, and smiled. "Have I told you yet this morning how much I love you?"

I sit at the edge of the bed, breathe Peter's name warm in his ear, and nudge his shoulder. He scratches his nose and makes sucking sounds. I nudge him again. He opens his eyes. "What? What's the matter?" He turns over on his back. "You okay?" The lines, wrinkles, and creases have crawled back into bed with him, snuck in while I was at the window. They have moved fast and re-settled deeper than before.

"The moon makes a sound," I say.

He stares at me for a moment, leans forward and kisses each breast, then falls back into his pillow. He sighs. "Yes, love, and the stars sound like tractors, don't they?"

"No," I say, "that's just it. They don't make any sound at all."

Peter swims back into his dream, the muscles in his shoulders and legs fighting to pull him into darker waters. He breathes through his mouth, measured and steady.

A chill slides up my back, and I feel around on the floor for the sheets and blanket. We've missed some things underneath the bed. More bedding and linens—soft, folded piles of cotton we didn't know were there. Embroidered dish towels and hankies. Slips and yellowed pinafores. In the morning, we will tear off the tape and repack the last box.

ANA'S END

NO, THIS ISN'T HOW SHE THOUGHT she would go. *Simple* passings ran in her family. Fast, well-placed shots to the heart, the kind most people claimed they'd take over any other way to die. This, Ana thought, this right here was too much, filled with all sorts of unpleasant, unnecessary details.

Her young father had taken a headache to bed early one evening, forgoing his after-dinner cigar, and gave his good breath to God by sunrise. A lifetime later, on a snowy January afternoon, her mother had fallen sideways off the piano bench, narrowly missing the hissing radiator. She hadn't been playing music at the time but was, instead, reaching for the jug of Mogen David she kept near the damper pedal. A tiny woman bent close to the floor, her body made a soft thud, her hair bobby-pin quiet, a knowing smile on her lips when Ana found her that said, "No worries, daughter. The good Lord will keep my glass full."

Now here lay Ana herself, face down on the bathroom tile of her apartment, her right cheek slowly absorbing those small squares into itself. One minute, she'd been sitting on the toilet, and the next, she wasn't, with no memory of the in-between. How was it, she wondered, that she felt nothing, couldn't connect to the arms and legs she couldn't see but knew must still be attached? What kind of nonsense was this?

This broken promise—the promise of a quick death—wasn't the first in Ana's life. There had been others: the promise made to her on the side of the road that her younger brother, Johnny, would come home whole from the war; the promise that artist Walter Eisenbauer would take her and her fresh Midwestern face to the gallery walls of New York City; that Anton Dietz would love her forever if she just let him touch her down there, just this once, in the alley alongside George's Ballroom; that because she was a smart girl, she wouldn't wind up spending more than 60 years behind a bar in her family's saloon, snapping beer caps and breathing in the stale, gray smoke of other people's stumbled lives.

She lay still, while the walls buzzed and rattled. Other tenants took showers and shaved, brushed their teeth, filled coffeemakers, stirred honey into their tea. Someone down the hall burned toast. But not enough, Ana thought disappointedly. Probably just one slice of bread. Had it been two slices, or something more substantial, like, say, a bagel, especially the kind with cinnamon sugar on top, the kind that can bubble and flare beside the heating coils in an instant, it might've triggered the smoke alarm. And that would've prompted the building to evacuate. And the fire department to come. And someone to make the rounds and search the individual units for unaccounted-for residents, the ones whose names hadn't been crossed off the list by the building manager when everyone gathered by the dumpsters.

"Did I ever tell you about the chickens?" a voice asked. "Those chickens we had in the basement? Did I ever tell you that story, Ana?"

Ana finished stocking the cooler under the bar and set a bottle of beer in front of Willy Kretsch. "Chickens? What, live ones?" she asked.

Willy nodded. "Back when Dad was just starting out, places couldn't always pay the band right away. They'd let the boys drink, a'course, much as they wanted, but the money wasn't there." He spun the base of his bottle back and forth on the polished wood with his thumb and middle finger, little stops and starts. "All the guys had families. They had to make a living, see. So they wound up taking chickens as payment. Least till the joints could make it right again, ya know, with cash."

Ana lit a cigarette and leaned against the back bar. She slowly rubbed the red, scaly underside of her arms. "And you kept them in the basement?"

Willy nodded again. "Middle a'winter in Minnesota, living in town, we didn't have a coop at the house. Couldn't leave 'em outside to freeze!" He chuckled. "Ma wasn't too happy. Dad'd come home late from a gig, chickens fussing and squawking in the car, shitting all over . . . A'course, he'd be three sheets to the wind that time a'night. 'Kretsch!' she'd yell, meeting him down the walk, the ends a'her scarf flapping behind her. 'What did I say about bringing home these *goddamn chickens*? Jesus Christ. Boys need boots. Willy lost his glasses again. We still owe at Doc Forstner's . . .' And Dad would hum some happy tune, shuffle past her, and weave his way across the yard to the side a'the house. Storm doors were right below my window, and he'd open 'em up, carry the cages into the cellar."

Ana blew smoke to the ceiling. "Then what?"

Willy took a long pull off his bottle, smacked his lips. "Well, then he'd go to bed and pass out, and the next day, Ma and Nick, my older brother, and I would have to go downstairs and kill 'em, a'course. We ate a lot a'chicken that winter, boy."

The bell over the front door jingled. In walked Tom and Weasel, regulars.

"Hey," Ana said, grabbing two beers from the cooler, "you two ever hear the story of Willy's chickens?"

"Heard the story of Willy's cock before, but not his chickens," Weasel said. He slid onto a red vinyl stool with a "hee, hee, hee" and dove his hand into a bowl of beer nuts.

"Says he killed chickens in his basement," Ana continued.

Tom set his cap on the bar. "Probably should've gotten an exterminator for that," he said.

"You sure they were chickens, Willy? Huh?" Weasel asked. "'Cause if they had long skinny tails and went 'squeak! squeak! squeak!' they weren't chickens!"

Willy shook his head. "No, when I was growing up. Telling Ana here I had to help butcher chickens my dad brought home. Ma and my brother, they did the cutting and dunked the bodies in hot water and all that."

"So then what the hell did *you* do, ya lazy sack of shit?" Tom asked.

"Sometimes they got away," Willy said, "and I had to go get 'em."

"Got away?"

"Yeah."

"Got away to where?"

"Well, sometimes, after their heads were cut off, the chickens would go running around the room." Willy tap-danced his fingers along the edge of the bar like scurrying bird legs.

Tom leaned backward and smiled. "Get out of here—"

"For some reason they always liked to run under the utility sink, and I was the only one small enough to crawl under there and grab 'em, so—"

"Fuckin' headless hens. In the goddamn basement," Tom said. "Willy, friend, you take the cake."

"I seen that a lot out on my grandpa's farm years ago," Weasel said through a mouthful of nuts. "Cut a chicken's head off, body doesn't know it's missing, and the chicken just keeps going. Runs around, flaps its wings—"

"*Ja*, I know that," Tom said. "They can live for a while without a brain. Just like you do every day." He snorted. "But in the basement of the house? Shit. No wonder Willy's so fucked up."

Ana shook her head and walked back to the grill area to check on her sauerkraut. She'd never seen a live chicken butchered in person, but she'd seen a TV program about it once—footage of a chicken, its head gone, springing from the block and sprinting full speed for the flock it couldn't see, the clucks it couldn't hear. How long, she wondered, before the chicken's brain realized it was on its own? The cameraman had focused on the spectacle of the body and its red spray, but what about the head? The head lying there alongside the chopping block? Were the hen's eyes blinking? Its beak clicking? How many breaths did it take before understanding that its lungs weren't attached anymore, but were instead ballooning 30, 40, 50 feet away?

Now footsteps. Keys. The simple piano chords of a soap opera theme song. A hacking cough let loose in the hall by a man too lazy to keep it tied up. Clacking dishes. Farm-market reports crackling over a radio. A violent sneeze repeated three times and finished with a "hoooo!"

Ana called out, still sprawled and numb on the bathroom floor. A voice—a clear, sturdy voice—outside an apartment a few doors down replied. Not to her, though.

"No, I understand, Ethel," it said. "I completely understand. You did the right thing. Don't worry about it. You just—you just have to—"

Ana couldn't make out the other end of the conversation, but she knew it was Larry Nixt, the building manager, talking to old Ethel Luehman in 4F.

"Yep, it's supposed to do that, that blinking. That's how you know it's working. If it starts beeping, Ethel, when it beeps, like a high-pitched chirp, then you give me a call, okay?" A pause, then Larry again. "What's that, now?" Another pause. "Oh, Ethel, you don't need to do that. You're a sweetheart. You're a real sweetheart."

Ana called out a second time. Or maybe not. Had her lips moved? She *thought* she'd heard her own words. Perhaps she'd only hummed.

Larry's voice grew louder, as if he were making his way to Ana's end of the hallway. "No, it's no trouble at all," he said. "That's what I get paid for."

"I love you, Larry!" Ethel shouted.

"Aw, c'mon, now, Ethel," Larry yelled back playfully, "you know I'm married! But if I weren't, I tell ya Love you, too, dear! You take care now!"

Larry's footsteps stopped outside Ana's door, and she held her breath. But there was no knock, just the whisper of an envelope slipping through the mail slot, and Larry's footsteps walking away with a whistle.

Ana's little brother, Johnny, just two years younger, had such beautiful hands, though Ana could never convince him of that fact. Long, thin fingers. Nails tapered and trimmed just so. "Piano hands" Ana called them. Holding up her own—her stubby sausage-fingers splayed—she often asked her mother why Johnny had gotten the pretty hands. Weren't girls supposed to be the pretty ones? Her mother, never breaking rhythm from her measuring, kneading, and crimping, would tell her daughter that when God gave out gifts, he gave out just one of two: beauty or intelligence. Not both. Johnny was handsome, and Ana was smart, the second-smartest in her class, and she should be grateful. Some people got no gifts at all.

"But no one sees 'smart,'" Ana said, playing with the measuring spoons. "No one asks 'smart' to the junior dance."

"*Hehr zu, Kind*. Listen. You have a good brain, *gel*? Poor Johnny—he struggles. It takes him time to catch up. So God gives him a handsome face. *Verstehst?* Now—*geh weg! Weg!* I'm busy here."

Ana shuffled to the kitchen door, picked at the white scabs on the undersides of her arms.

"Ana," her mother continued, "toilets need cleaning for tonight. And—ach—stop scratching! You make it worse." The kitchen timer dinged. "Don't be such a buck. Tuck in that bottom lip, or—"

"Or a bird'll come and poop on it," Ana said before letting the screen door slam behind her. "I know, Ma. I know."

Ana walked heavily down the open wooden stairs leading from her family's rooms to the saloon below, letting her full weight drop with each footfall. Never mind, she thought, that her own mother had just confirmed she was ugly. And never mind the boys at school who never looked her way. She'd take

Johnny to next week's dance, like always. Sweet, quiet Johnny, with his soft white-blond curls, blue eyes, and downy baby face, willing to do whatever his older sister asked.

At dances and other school and church functions, the two were tethered. He'd take her coat, fetch her drinks, fill her dance card. She'd loop her arm in his and pull him tight whenever other girls circled, tongues wagging. Part of her glowed, loved knowing that she had what the popular girls wanted. Another part of her stiffened territorially, like a shadowed dog beneath the porch. When they weren't doing chores for their mother in the saloon, Ana and Johnny got ice creams together downtown, helped clean and fix frames for the Portners' hives along the Minnesota River, scouted deer tracks in the sand. Wherever one sibling went, the other usually followed. Years later, after Johnny returned from the war and moved back in with his mother and sister, took up his old bartending job, folks new to town often asked him about his delightful wife, Ana—that sassy, beer-pouring spitfire—and said what a perfect couple they made, that you could really feel how much they loved each other. And in those moments, the regulars, perched on their stools, quietly lost themselves in the polish of the bar, the picking of bottle labels, while Johnny politely set the strangers right.

Ana filled a bucket with hot water and wheeled the cart around to the women's restroom. She cleaned the toilet bowl, wiped down the mirror and sink, and scrubbed the tile floor on her hands and knees. Once done she closed the door and locked herself inside.

She undid the top three buttons of her blouse and unpinned her bun. When she asked the mirror her question, knowing it couldn't lie, it answered plainly: long auburn hair, whiskey-straight and fine, ruddy cheeks, eyes dark as molasses.

Ana sighed. Her mother had spoken true about God doling out just one gift or the other. Clearly Ana's wasn't beauty. But He *had* thrown her a bone. She reached into the deep pocket of her skirt and pulled out the red lipstick she'd found in the women's restroom a few weekends ago. As measured and careful as prayer, she painted her lips—first the small right wing of the upper lip, then the left, then the long, plump bottom line, the lipstick tugging gently as she drew it across. She admired her work for a moment—the wet red bow, promising a gift— then kissed the air. She closed her eyes, slipped the fingers of one hand past the unbuttoned buttons, while the fingers of the other traced her lips, teased open her mouth. Ana was smart, and she had these lips, these full, God-given lips, the same lips as her beautiful brother's. But, Ana thought, with a mixture of sadness and happiness, Johnny's were better. Johnny's were softer.

Ana's right eye wouldn't open. Or maybe it was open but had gone blind from the fall. She couldn't tell. Her left eye—cloaked in cataract—comforted her, kept the room soft. The white bathroom tiles, so intimate now with her face and body, looked like squares of fresh snow, each edge rounded over into the grout, drifted smooth. Ana didn't feel the heat register exhale. A strand of hair caught on her eyelashes did. It wagged. She watched the hair, unblinking, until the apartment reached 68 degrees. Then the wagging stopped.

"Honest to God, Father, I died," Ana said. "Died same as him. February 19, 1971." She shook her head slowly at the priest, wringing her hands. "Couldn't wake him. He wouldn't wake up. I called his name. Called it, and called it. Shook him. Shook him hard as I could, but . . . Ma was sitting in the corner of his room, sitting and praying the rosary—just praying I don't know how long."

Johnny hadn't kept his promise; he hadn't come home whole from the war in Germany. To anyone but family, the golden boy looked unchanged, with his open face, easy smile, and sure, lean hands slinging drinks. But Ana saw them right away, the shadows that crouched quiet outside the blue of his eyes and waited, waited for the door to crack open just enough for them to slip inside with their hooks. Ana threw herself at that door, pushed against it with all her weight, knowing full well Johnny didn't have strength to do it himself, that their mother would be too meek. And Ana held it strong damn-near 30 years.

Ana and Johnny spent every day and night teamed behind the bar—Ana igniting the patrons with her crude jokes and fiery lips, Johnny pouring and mixing and drinking and wondering at his sister's bright light. She drank and smoked with him, cooked for him, hung his clothes on the line, woke him in the morning with cups of black coffee.

"But God didn't make me smart enough," Ana said. "Not for those demons. Something, *gel*, how a person can be so close to someone, love someone so much, yet not able to do a goddamn thing."

Days before his 49th birthday, Ana found her brother in the basement, gaunt and yellowed among the wooden crates and cockroaches. Tucked in a corner, he was soaked through, from his matted hair to the seat of his pants. A cocktail of sweat, piss, and beer. He'd been slipping over the past few months, detaching, finding ways to hide in plain sight. There, but not there. Ana had never seen him so bad and asked what he was doing in the basement. He shook her off. When she asked a second time, he looked up, and she saw the door she'd tried so hard to hold had been ripped off its hinges, the shadows already anchored deep inside his eyes.

"I can't do it anymore, Ana," he told her. He wiped the corner of his mouth with the back of his hand. His breath hitched. "I'm broken."

Ana reached out. "Let's go upstairs and get you cleaned up. *Gel*?" She nodded toward the steps. "I'll run a bath. Get you something to eat."

Johnny didn't move, didn't blink. "I let you down," he said quietly. "And I'm so sorry."

Ana's chest tightened. She bit down hard on the inside of her lip and cleared her throat. "You haven't had more than a couple pieces of toast since Monday," she said. "You just need a good, hot meal. That's what you need. And some rest. C'mon, give me your hand." Then lowering her voice and leaning close, "Give me your hand, *Schatz*. Let's go up. C'mon now."

Johnny looked down into his lap, into his open, empty palms. Ana didn't know what he saw there, cupped by those long fingers, but whatever it was, he held it with adoration.

Ana nodded. "Okay. Okay. You come up when you're ready, then, *gel*?" She picked up a case of beer and started hauling it up the stairs. "I'll have Ma get some soup going," she said, looking back over her shoulder. "Maybe make some dumplings."

In the darkened corner, her brother curled tighter into himself, squeezed his head between his hands, and cried.

Father Fritsche had just come yesterday, so he wouldn't be back for another week. Ana didn't subscribe to the paper, didn't shop from catalogs or the Internet, and her mail was dropped through a slot in her door—nothing to collect outside her apartment. She didn't play Sheephead, wasn't a member of the Ladies' Auxiliary, or the quilting club. Didn't receive Meals on Wheels. Didn't have a pet. Although she'd served thousands of people through the years at the saloon before selling the building, she had no friends to check on her. No family left. No voice. No feeling. No sense of awake and asleep.

The snow continued to pile up before her eyes. So much powdery snow stretched out before her, as far as she could see. Magnificent, really. She ran through it, kicked great white sprays behind her with her heels and felt the crystals kiss the nape of her neck and slide inside her collar, down her back to the hooks of her bra. She opened her mouth, laughed, and tasted that sweet, cold sugar on her tongue. Everything before her was white. Every last thing. Everywhere Ana looked.

ACKNOWLEDGMENTS

To my mom and dad, Lois "Toots" and Roger Kalz, for patiently supporting and loving your adventuresome, overachieving, book-obsessed, moon-gazing band geek of a daughter (me) and letting me make mistakes and fail so I could grow.

To my brother, Mike, for his always-entertaining, often-irreverent dinner-table storytelling; his ability to attract the most colorful characters at any bar; and for downsizing my ego whenever it ceases to fit through doorways.

To my editor, Nicole Helget, whose trust and on-point editorial suggestions nudged me to dig deeper and made this book richer for it. Thank you for taking good care of my kids.

To Brian and Deborah Fors of Minneopa Valley Press, Inc., for giving *The Winter Bees* a nurturing hive in which to live.

To the Prairie Lakes Regional Arts Council, the McKnight Foundation, Ragdale, and the Anderson Center of Interdisciplinary Arts, for the gifts of time and space within which to write.

To Rick Apitz, for stopping time and starting stories with his Nikons and Canons.

To my teachers, for their encouragement and unwavering high expectations throughout school and beyond, especially Charlotte Anderson, Terry Davis, Ingrid

Liedman, Rick Robbins, Jan Senst, and Roger Sheffer. Profound thanks to Eddie Micus, because without the poetry (and its many moons), I would have no prose.

To the many ghosts of the no-longer-with-us Kalz's Corner of New Ulm, Minnesota, whom I hope I've served well with this book.

And finally, to Steve Martin and Bill Murray. Just because.

Author Photo by Rick Apitz

JILL KALZ lives and writes in New Ulm, Minnesota. She has published poetry in the *Nebraska Review*, the *Ohio Review*, *Cream City Review*, and other magazines. Her short stories have appeared in *American Fiction Vol. 15* and *Minnesota Monthly*. A 2008 Minnesota Book Award finalist and winner of the Readers' Choice Award for her picture book *Farmer Cap*, Kalz is also the author of more than 70 children's books. She holds an MFA in creative writing from Minnesota State University, Mankato, and works as a children's book editor.